A BARTIMAEUS GRAPHIC NOVEL

The Amulet of Samarkand

ADAPTED BY
JONATHAN STROUD
AND ANDREW DONKIN

ART BY
LEE SULLIVAN

COLOR BY
NICOLAS CHAPUIS

LETTERING BY
CHRIS DICKEY

DISNEY · HYPERION BOOKS
New York

Adapted from the Bartimaeus novel *The Amulet of Samarkand*

Text copyright © 2010 by Jonathan Stroud
Illustrations copyright © 2010 by Lee Sullivan

Printed in the United States of America
F322-8368-0-10213
First Edition
10 9 8 7 6 5 4 3 2 1
ISBN: 978-1-4231-1146-7 (hardcover)
Library of Congress Cataloging-in-Publication Data on file.
ISBN: 978-1-4231-1147-4 (paperback)
Library of Congress Catalog
Card Number on file.

Visit www.HyperionBooksForChildren.com

Certified Chain of Custody
SUSTAINABLE   35% Certified Forests,
FORESTRY   65% Certified Fiber Sourcing
INITIATIVE
www.sfiprogram.org

LONDON.
NOW.

"Above all, there is one fact that we must drive into your wretched little skull now so that you never forget it."

"Yes, sir."

"Do you know what that fact is?"

"No, sir."

"No? Well then, boy, I shall tell you. It is this. Demons are very, very wicked. They will hurt you if they can. Do you understand?"

"Yes, sir."

TRAFALGAR SQUARE

NORTH GATE

DEVEREAUX BUILDING

ONE WORLD EXHIBITION

BUMPO THE BEAR'S GROTTO OF TAXIDERMY

HOG ROAST

KEEP OFF THE GRASS

"Are you sure, boy?"

"Yes, sir. I understand. Demons are very, very wicked and will hurt you if they can."

EVENING EDITION. LATEST NEWS!

AAARKK!

AAARKK!

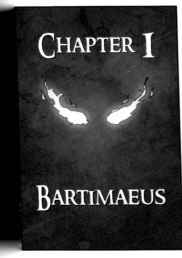

CHAPTER I

BARTIMAEUS

THE TEMPERATURE OF THE ROOM DROPPED FAST. ICE FORMED ON THE CURTAINS AND CANDLES.

KRRACKLE

THE ROOM FILLED WITH A YELLOW, CHOKING CLOUD OF BRIMSTONE.

INDISTINCT BLACK SHADOWS WRITHED AND ROILED INSIDE IT.

THE CLOUD FORMED TENDRILS THAT LICKED THE AIR LIKE HUNGRY TONGUES.

SCHLUURPP

SCHLUURPP

INVISIBLE FEET PATTERED ACROSS FLOORBOARDS, AND INVISIBLE MOUTHS WHISPERED WICKED THINGS FROM BEHIND THE BED AND UNDER THE DESK.

THUB

THUB THUB

FROM FAR AWAY CAME THE SOUND OF MANY VOICES SCREAMING...

AAAIIEEE!

HEY, IT WAS HIS FIRST TIME.

I WANTED TO SCARE HIM.

FZZZT

FZZZT

FZZZT

I DID, TOO.

I CHARGE YOU... TO...TO T-T-TELL ME YOUR NAME.

HE KNEW AND I KNEW THAT HE KNEW MY NAME ALREADY.

I AM BARTIMAEUS.

OTHERWISE, HOW COULD HE HAVE SUMMONED ME IN THE FIRST PLACE? YOU NEED THE RIGHT WORDS, THE RIGHT ACTIONS, AND MOST OF ALL, THE RIGHT NAME.

I SAW HIM GIVE A GULP. GOOD, HE KNEW MY REPUTATION.

ARE YOU THAT BARTIMAEUS WHO IN OLDEN TIMES WAS SUMMONED BY THE MAGICIANS TO REPAIR THE WALLS OF PRAGUE AND WHO DID—

WHAT A TIME WASTER THIS KID WAS.

I UPPED THE VOLUME A BIT ON THIS ONE.

I AM BARTIMAEUS! I AM SAKHR AL-JINNI, N'GORSO THE MIGHTY, AND SERPENT OF SILVER PLUMES! I HAVE REBUILT THE WALLS OF URUK, KARNAK, AND PRAGUE. I HAVE SPOKEN WITH SOLOMON. I HAVE WATCHED OVER OLD ZIMBABWE TILL THE STONES FELL AND THE JACKALS FED ON ITS PEOPLE.

I AM BARTIMAEUS! I RECOGNIZE NO MASTER! SO I CHARGE YOU, **BOY**. WHO ARE YOU TO SUMMON ME?

IMPRESSIVE STUFF, EH? ALL TRUE AS WELL, WHICH GAVE IT EVEN MORE POWER.

I RATHER HOPED HE WOULD BE BLUSTERED INTO TELLING ME HIS NAME OR STEPPING OUTSIDE THE CIRCLE SO I COULD NAB HIM.

NO LUCK THERE, THEN.

BY THE CONSTRAINTS OF THE CIRCLE, THE POINTS ON THE PENTACLE, AND THE CHAIN OF RUNES, I AM YOUR MASTER!

YOU WILL OBEY ME!

I MUST ADMIT I WAS ALREADY SURPRISED. YOU DON'T OFTEN GET SMALL ONES LIKE THIS SQUIRT CALLING UP AN EXTRAORDINARILY POWERFUL AND MODEST ENTITY LIKE MYSELF.

ANYTHING TO GET THIS OVER WITH QUICKLY.

WHAT IS YOUR WILL?

I WAITED GRIMLY FOR THE PATHETIC REQUEST. LEVITATING SOME TATTY OBJECT WAS A USUAL ONE. OR MOVING IT AROUND THE ROOM A BIT.

PERHAPS HE'D WANT ME TO CONJURE AN ILLUSION. THAT MIGHT BE FUN. THERE WAS BOUND TO BE A WAY OF MISINTERPRETING HIS REQUEST.

ONCE, A MAGICIAN DEMANDED I SHOW HIM THE LOVE OF HIS LIFE. I RUSTLED UP A MIRROR.

WELL, BOY?

I CHARGE YOU TO RETRIEVE THE AMULET OF SAMARKAND FROM THE HOUSE OF SIMON LOVELACE AND BRING IT TO ME WHEN I SUMMON YOU AT DAWN TOMORROW.

IT WAS PEEING WITH NOVEMBER RAIN.

JUST MY LUCK.

I HAD TAKEN THE FORM OF A BLACKBIRD, AND WITHIN SECONDS I WAS AS BEDRAGGLED A FOWL AS EVER HUNCHED ITS WINGS IN HAMPSTEAD.

THE VILLAS OPPOSITE LOOKED LIKE THE FACES OF THE DEAD. OR PERHAPS IT WAS JUST MY MOOD.

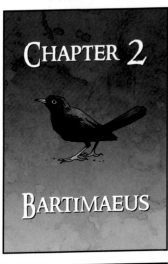

CHAPTER 2

BARTIMAEUS

FIVE THINGS WERE BOTHERING ME.

FOR A START, THE DULL ACHE THAT COMES WITH EVERY PHYSICAL MANIFESTATION WAS ALREADY BEGINNING. I COULD FEEL IT IN MY FEATHERS.

THE SECOND THING WAS THE WEATHER.

ENOUGH SAID.

THIRD, I'D FORGOTTEN THE LIMITATIONS OF MATERIAL BODIES. I HAD AN ITCH JUST ABOVE MY BEAK THAT I COULDN'T REACH TO SCRATCH.

FOURTH, THAT KID.

WHO WAS HE, AND WHY DID HE HAVE A DEATH WISH?

FIFTH ... THE AMULET. WHAT THE KID THOUGHT HE WAS GOING TO DO WITH IT WAS ANYONE'S GUESS.

I HAD TO STEAL IT FIRST, THOUGH, AND THAT WOULD NOT NECESSARILY BE EASY, EVEN FOR ME.

CHAPTER 3

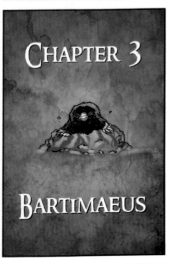

BARTIMAEUS

THE TASTE OF MUD IS NO FIT THING FOR A BEING OF AIR AND FIRE.

BUT THERE'S NO POINT BEING FASTIDIOUS WHEN YOU HAVE A PROTECTIVE SHIELD TO BYPASS.

I AM CHOOSY ABOUT MY INCARNATIONS.

BIRDS, GOOD. INSECTS, GOOD. BATS, OKAY. THINGS THAT RUN FAST ARE FINE. TREE DWELLERS ARE EVEN BETTER. SUBTERRANEAN THINGS, NOT GOOD.

MOLES, BAD.

IT WILL BE THE MOST MAGNIFICENT OCCASION, AMANDA. YOU WILL BE THE TOAST OF LONDON SOCIETY...

WITH SOME RELIEF, I BECAME A FLY.

TWO HUMANS WERE SITTING UNDERNEATH A HIDEOUS CRYSTAL THING THAT WAS PRETENDING TO BE A CHANDELIER.

AND YOU'RE SURE THE PRIME MINISTER WILL COME?

AMANDA, HE IS VERY MUCH LOOKING FORWARD TO VIEWING YOUR ESTATE.

I MEMORIZED THE WOMAN INSTANTLY. I WOULD APPEAR IN HER GUISE TOMORROW WHEN I WENT BACK TO VISIT THAT KID. ONLY NAKED. LET'S SEE HOW HIS ADOLESCENT MIND COPED WITH THAT.

CHAPTER 4

BARTIMAEUS

ON THE SECOND PLANE, I SAW AN IMP FLOATING OVER LOVELACE'S SHOULDER ON THE LOOKOUT FOR DANGER.

EVEN WITH YOUR MANY RIVALS HOUNDING HIM THESE LAST FEW WEEKS?

DESPITE THEIR CONSTANT EFFORTS TO HAVE IT MOVED, HE HAS REMAINED COMMITTED TO HOLDING THE CONFERENCE AT YOUR DELIGHTFUL HALL.

YOU'VE ALWAYS KNOWN HOW TO PLAY THE P.M., SIMON. HOW TO FLATTER HIS VANITY.

IT WAS A PITY I WASN'T A SPIDER. THEY CAN SIT FOR HOURS.

FLIES ARE MORE JITTERY, AND I HAD TO FORCE MY UNWILLING BODY TO LURK.

KEEP IT TO YOURSELF, MY LOVE, BUT ALL HE REALLY HAS LEFT NOW IS CHARM, AND MOST DAYS HE DOESN'T EVEN BOTHER WITH THAT.

PARDON ME SIR, BUT THE CARS ARE READY.

IT PAINS ME, AMANDA, BUT DUTY CALLS. I MUST RETURN TO PARLIAMENT.

MY GOOD FRIEND MAKEPEACE HAS SENT THE TICKETS FOR HIS PLAY, SO I SHALL SEE YOU AT THE THEATER TOMORROW EVENING.

BEHIND ME I HEARD DOORS SLAM. PERFECT. I'D MUCH RATHER THE MASTER MAGICIAN WASN'T HOME WHEN I BORROWED HIS AMULET.

FOLLOWING AN INTUITION, I HEADED UPSTAIRS.

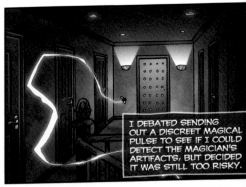

I DEBATED SENDING OUT A DISCREET MAGICAL PULSE TO SEE IF I COULD DETECT THE MAGICIAN'S ARTIFACTS, BUT DECIDED IT WAS STILL TOO RISKY.

ON THE LANDING, I SPIED ONE DOOR THAT WAS REINFORCED WITH STEEL.

THE FLY DISSOLVED INTO A DRIBBLE OF SMOKE.

IN THE ROOM, I BECAME A CHILD.

SOMEONE I HAD LOVED. HIS DUST HAD LONG AGO FLOATED AWAY ALONG THE NILE.

THERE WERE SEVERAL CABINETS FULL OF MAGICAL PARAPHERNALIA.

MOST OF IT QUITE USELESS.

fit only for stage show

tat → more tat

rubbish

looted

Lovelace's "Treasures"

BLOOD

looks old but probably made last week in a factory in Catford

nicked tat

stolen

BUT NOT ALL OF IT WAS TAT.

THERE WAS A SUMMONING HORN SO POWERFUL IT MADE ME FEEL SICK TO LOOK AT IT.

THERE WAS AN EYE MADE OUT OF CLAY.

I'D SEEN THOSE FIRSTHAND IN PRAGUE. I WONDERED IF THE FOOL KNEW ITS POTENTIAL.

AND THERE WAS THE AMULET OF SAMARKAND. PROTECTED BY A SMALL CASE AND ITS OWN REPUTATION.

IT HAD LAIN BURIED IN THE TOMB OF A PRINCESS FOR THREE THOUSAND YEARS UNTIL IT WAS FOUND BY ARCHAEOLOGISTS AND THEN STOLEN BY MAGICIANS.

I COCKED MY HEAD AGAIN, LISTENING.

ALL WAS QUIET IN THE HOUSE.

I CLENCHED MY FIST AND DROVE IT THROUGH THE GLASS.

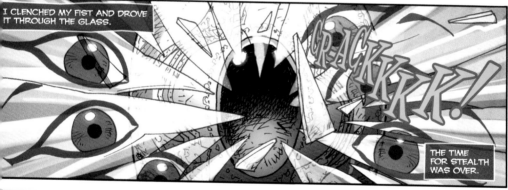

CRACKKKKK!

THE TIME FOR STEALTH WAS OVER.

MAGICAL ALARMS WENT OFF ON ALL SEVEN PLANES. A PORTAL OPENED BEHIND ME AND SOMETHING STEPPED THROUGH. IT BEGAN FIRING DETONATIONS.

CRACKKKKK!

KA-BOOM!

KA-BOOM!

I HIT THE DOOR WITH MY SMALL BOY FIST, AND IT SHATTERED BEFORE ME.

"Above all, there is one fact that we must drive into your wretched little skull now so that you never forget it."

"Yes, sir."

"Do you know what that fact is?"

"No, sir."

"No? Well then, boy, I shall tell you. It is this. Demons are very, very wicked. They will hurt you if they can. Do you understand?"

"Yes, sir."

I cannot stop watching his eyebrows.

ARE YOU SURE, BOY?

YES, SIR. I UNDERSTAND. DEMONS ARE VERY, VERY WICKED AND WILL HURT YOU IF THEY CAN.

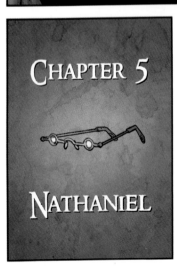

CHAPTER 5

NATHANIEL

WELL NOW, YOU SAY YES, AND I AM SURE YOU MEAN YES — AND YET...

I DO NOT FEEL CONVINCED THAT YOU REALLY, TRULY UNDERSTAND.

"Go to my study, boy. On my desk is a box. In the box is a pair of spectacles. Put them on and come back to me. Simple, yes?"

I had never been allowed in this room before.

STOP! B-... BEGONE!

Then I remembered the spectacles.

It was twenty minutes before he came to get me. It was a week before I could speak again.

I was six years old at the time.

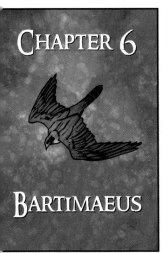

CHAPTER 6

BARTIMAEUS

I FLEW FROM HAMPSTEAD AT TOP SPEED AND TOOK SHELTER UNDER THE EAVES OF A DESERTED HOUSE BY THE THAMES.

I PREENED MY FEATHERS AND WATCHED THE SKY.

AS I EXPECTED, THE MAGICIAN SENT OUT SEARCH SPHERES TO HUNT DOWN HIS AMULET.

ONE OF THE PROBLEMS WITH POWERFUL MAGICAL ARTIFACTS IS THAT THEY HAVE A DISTINCTIVE PULSATING AURA THAT'S ABOUT AS SUBTLE AS A NAKED MAN AT A FUNERAL.

I KNEW I HAD TO KEEP MOVING.

SO I CONTINUED MY FRANTIC, FUGITIVE DANCE ACROSS LONDON. THE URCHIN HAD FORBIDDEN ME TO RETURN BEFORE DAWN AND I WOULD BE EXHAUSTED LONG BEFORE THAT.

LONDON

I DECIDED ON A NEW PLAN. I WOULD DROWN OUT THE AMULET'S PULSE BY MINGLING WITH THE GREAT UNWASHED — IN OTHER WORDS, WITH PEOPLE.

I WAS THAT DESPERATE.

EVEN AT THIS HOUR, TRAFALGAR SQUARE WAS BUSY. LATE-NIGHT CUSTOMERS WERE OUT BUYING CUT-PRICE CHARMS FROM THE OFFICIAL BOOTHS.

AROUND THE SQUARE, CAR LIGHTS SWIRLED, VEHICLES CARRYING MINISTERS AND OTHER MAGICIANS TO THEIR OFFICES IN PARLIAMENT.

I WAS NEAR THE HUB OF A GREAT WHEEL OF POWER THAT EXTENDED OVER AN EMPIRE.

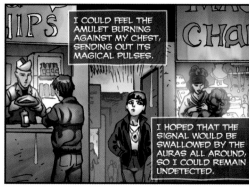

I COULD FEEL THE AMULET BURNING AGAINST MY CHEST, SENDING OUT ITS MAGICAL PULSES.

I HOPED THAT THE SIGNAL WOULD BE SWALLOWED BY THE AURAS ALL AROUND, SO I COULD REMAIN UNDETECTED.

A FEW MOMENTS LATER I HAD THE UNEASY FEELING THAT I WAS BEING WATCHED.

I CHECKED ALL THE PLANES. NO HIDDEN DANGERS.

THEN THE FEELING CAME AGAIN. I SWIVELED QUICKER THAN A CAT AND...

I CAUGHT THE STARERS EYEBALL TO EYEBALL.

THE GIRL'S EYES WERE COLD AND HARD. I GAZED BACK. WHAT DID I CARE? THEY WERE HUMAN; THEY COULDN'T SEE WHAT I WAS. LET THEM STARE.

WHEN I MOVED OFF, THE CHILDREN FOLLOWED ME.

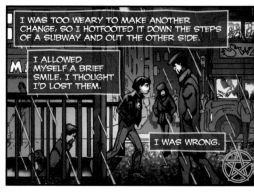

I WAS TOO WEARY TO MAKE ANOTHER CHANGE, SO I HOTFOOTED IT DOWN THE STEPS OF A SUBWAY AND OUT THE OTHER SIDE.

I ALLOWED MYSELF A BRIEF SMILE. I THOUGHT I'D LOST THEM.

I WAS WRONG.

CHAPTER 7

BARTIMAEUS

THE OLD PAIN HAD STARTED UP AGAIN, THROBBING IN MY STOMACH AND THROUGH MY BONES. IT WASN'T HEALTHY TO BE ENCASED IN A PHYSICAL BODY FOR SO LONG.

THE AMULET BEAT AGAINST MY CHEST WITH EVERY STEP. I WOULD HAVE HAPPILY LOBBED IT INTO THE NEAREST TRASH CAN, BUT I WAS BOUND BY MY ORDERS FROM THAT KID.

THE MASSED DARKNESS OF THE HIGH BUILDINGS CLOSED IN ON EITHER SIDE, OPPRESSING ME.

CITIES GET ME DOWN, ALMOST AS IF I WERE UNDERGROUND.

THEY MAKE ME LONG FOR THE SOUTH.

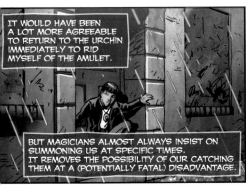

IT WOULD HAVE BEEN A LOT MORE AGREEABLE TO RETURN TO THE URCHIN IMMEDIATELY TO RID MYSELF OF THE AMULET.

BUT MAGICIANS ALMOST ALWAYS INSIST ON SUMMONING US AT SPECIFIC TIMES. IT REMOVES THE POSSIBILITY OF OUR CATCHING THEM AT A (POTENTIALLY FATAL) DISADVANTAGE.

THE BOY WOULD PAY FOR THIS. YOU DIDN'T REDUCE BARTIMAEUS OF URUK TO DOSSING IN DOORWAYS AND GET AWAY WITH IT.

THEN I HEARD SOMETHING. FOOTSTEPS IN THE ALLEY.

IT WAS THE CHILDREN FROM TRAFALGAR SQUARE WITH THE GIRL AT THEIR HEAD.

I CAST A SOPHISTICATED CONCEALMENT UPON MYSELF.

A LAYER OF TIGHTLY LACED PURPLE THREADS COVERED ME, RENDERING ME UTTERLY INVISIBLE.

IT'S THERE.

GET IT.

OOPS.

I WAS OVERWHELMED BY A TIDAL WAVE OF DISTRESSED LEATHER, CHEAP AFTERSHAVE, AND BODY ODOR.

BUT I AM BARTIMAEUS, AND I LET LOOSE A BRIEF DISCHARGE OF HEAT AND LIGHT THAT SHOULD HAVE REDUCED THE BOYS TO CHARRED CORPSES...

...BUT SOMEHOW DIDN'T. MY MAGIC SEEMED NOT TO AFFECT THESE CHILDREN AT ALL.

YOU HAVE SOMETHING AROUND YOUR NECK.

SAYS WHO?

IT'S BEEN IN FULL VIEW FOR THE LAST TWO MINUTES, YOU CRETIN.

OH. FAIR ENOUGH.

YOU'RE NOT A MAGICIAN.

TOO RIGHT, I'M NOT! WOULD A MAGICIAN DO SO WELL AGAINST YOUR WICKEDNESS?

SHE HAD A POINT THERE. EVEN WITH A DOZEN CHARMS, AN ARMY OF IMPS, AND A HEAVYWEIGHT DJINNI, A MAGICIAN WOULD HAVE HAD A JOB SUBDUING THE GREAT BARTIMAEUS.

THIS GIRL AND HER BOYFRIENDS HAD DONE IT ALL ON THEIR OWN, WITHOUT SEEMING PARTICULARLY FUSSED.

THE UNDERWOOD HOUSE, HIGHGATE.

BEFORE.

I REALLY DO NOT SEE WHY WE HAVE TO HAVE THE CHILD ACTUALLY LIVING IN THE HOUSE, MARTHA.

YOU MIGHT ENJOY IT, DEAR.

I AM NOT GOING TO ENJOY IT.

AND THESE EGGS ARE TOO RUNNY AGAIN.

SORRY, DEAR.

CHAPTER 8

NATHANIEL

I HAVE NEVER HAD AN APPRENTICE AND I DO NOT WANT ONE.

HE'S ASLEEP AT LAST. IT WOULDN'T SURPRISE ME IF HE WAS IN SHOCK. I THINK IT'S DISGRACEFUL, RIPPING A CHILD AWAY FROM HIS HOME SO YOUNG.

APPRENTICES HAVE TO COME FROM SOMEWHERE, MARTHA. ANYWAY, APPARENTLY HIS PARENTS COULDN'T GET AWAY FAST ENOUGH. TOOK THE MONEY AND RAN.

IT'S A SITUATION WHERE EVERYONE WINS. HIS FAMILY GETS A CONSIDERABLE AMOUNT OF MONEY AS COMPENSATION. HE GETS THE CHANCE TO SERVE HIS COUNTRY AT THE HIGHEST LEVEL.

AND THE STATE GETS A NEW APPRENTICE WHO IN TIME WILL LEARN TO BE A MAGICIAN AND SERVE THE EMPIRE.

WELL, I THINK HE SHOULD BE ALLOWED TO STAY WITH HIS FAMILY. OR AT LEAST SEE THEM SOMETIMES.

YOU KNOW THAT'S QUITE IMPOSSIBLE.

HIS BIRTH NAME MUST BE UTTERLY, UTTERLY FORGOTTEN.

NOW, DEAR, LET'S MAKE A DEAL. I KNOW YOU'VE BEEN TOLD NOT TO TELL ANYONE YOUR NAME, BUT YOU CAN TELL ME. I CAN'T KEEP CALLING YOU "BOY," CAN I?

SO IF YOU TELL ME YOUR NAME, I'LL TELL YOU MINE – IN STRICTEST CONFIDENCE. WHAT DO YOU THINK? I'M MARTHA. AND YOU ARE...

HE TOLD ME. HIS NAME'S NATHANIEL.

MARTHA!

YOU KNOWING HIS BIRTH NAME ONLY PUTS HIM IN DANGER FROM HIS ENEMIES.

HE HASN'T GOT ANY ENEMIES, DEAR. HE'S FIVE YEARS OLD.

WHY DO I HAVE TO SPEND ALL OUR ART LESSONS COPYING PATTERNS?

"I'd rather be drawing the house or the tree..."

...OR YOU, MS. LUTYENS.

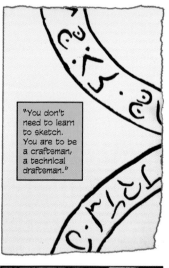

"You don't need to learn to sketch. You are to be a craftsman, a technical draftsman."

YOU MUST BE ABLE TO REPRODUCE ANY SEQUENCE OF SYMBOLS QUICKLY, CONFIDENTLY, AND ABOVE ALL, ACCURATELY.

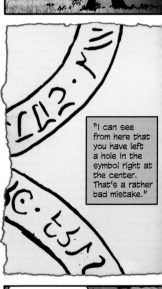

"I can see from here that you have left a hole in the symbol right at the center. That's a rather bad mistake."

IT'S ONLY A SMALL MISTAKE. THE REST IS OKAY, ISN'T IT?

"If you were using that design in a pentacle, that gap could cost you your life."

YOU DON'T WANT TO DIE JUST YET, DO YOU?

"I like it out here in the garden, Ms. Lutyens. It helps me think."

"He keeps me company."

"Gladstone?"

"I expect you learn about him in your history lessons. England's most powerful magician. He dominated the Empire for thirty years and made London the magical capital of the whole world. For better or worse."

WHAT DO YOU MEAN "FOR BETTER OR WORSE"? WHAT WAS WORSE ABOUT IT?

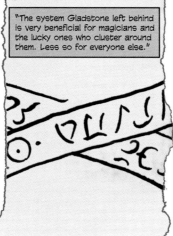

"The system Gladstone left behind is very beneficial for magicians and the lucky ones who cluster around them. Less so for everyone else."

WITHOUT MAGICIANS, MR. PURCELL SAYS THIS COUNTRY WOULD BE DEFENSELESS. AND THAT IT WOULD FALL APART IF THE COMMONERS WERE IN CHARGE.

"Commoners like me, you mean?"

"Sorry, Ms. Lutyens."

CHAPTER 9

BARTIMAEUS

IN THE END, DAWN CAME.

THE WHOLE OF THE NIGHT HAD BEEN WEARISOME AND I WAITED IMPATIENTLY FOR THE SUMMONS.

I WAS NOW ON THE ROOF OF WESTMINSTER ABBEY PRETENDING TO BE A GARGOYLE. THINGS DON'T GET MUCH WORSE THAN THAT.

I ALLOWED MYSELF A SHORT, LUXURIOUS FLEX OF MY WINGS.

AND AT THAT MOMENT, THE SUMMONS CAME. A THOUSAND PAINFUL FISHHOOKS SEEMED TO EMBED THEMSELVES IN ME.

I SUBMITTED IMMEDIATELY. I WISHED ONLY TO HAND OVER THE AMULET...

...AND BE DONE.

I ORDER YOU, BARTIMAEUS, TO REVEAL WHETHER YOU HAVE DILIGENTLY AND--

OF COURSE I HAVE - WHAT DO YOU THINK THIS IS?

IT WAS SIMON LOVELACE'S. NOW IT IS YOURS. SOON IT WILL BE SIMON LOVELACE'S AGAIN.

TAKE IT AND ENJOY THE CONSEQUENCES.

I MADE A BIG SHOW OF CHECKING THE LINES OF THE CIRCLE.

AHA! YOU'VE SPELLED THIS WRONG! AND YOU KNOW WHAT THAT MEANS!

THE KID'S FACE WENT AN INTERESTING MIX OF WHITE AND RED AS HE STUDIED THE LINES HIMSELF.

RECREANT DEMON! THE PENTACLE IS SOUND – IT BINDS YOU STILL!

OKAY, I LIED. NOW DO YOU WANT THIS OR NOT?

I WATCHED HIM CLOSELY. IF ONE FOOT OR ONE FINGER FELL OUTSIDE THE CIRCLE, I WOULD BE ON HIM FASTER THAN A PRAYING MANTIS. SADLY, HE PRODUCED A STICK.

EUCH, THIS IS DISGUSTING!

BLAME ROTHERHITHE SEWAGE WORKS AND THE DEMONIC HORDES OF LONDON THAT WERE CHASING ME.

YOU WERE PURSUED?

YOU SOUND ALMOST PLEASED. WRONG EMOTION, KID. TRY FEAR.

WELL, NO MATTER. I HAVE CARRIED OUT MY CHARGE. MY TASK IS DONE. FOR THE REMAINDER OF YOUR SHORT LIFE, FAREWELL!

YOU CANNOT DEPART! I HAVE OTHER WORK FOR THEE. ADELBRAND'S PENTACLE HOLDS YOU AT MY COMMAND.

MORE THAN THE RENEWED CAPTIVITY, IT WAS THE OCCASIONAL ARCHAISMS THAT ANNOYED ME SO MUCH. I ASK YOU... "THEE" AND "RECREANT DEMON"?!

BARTIMAEUS, I CHARGE YOU TO TAKE THE AMULET OF SAMARKAND AND HIDE IT IN THE MAGICAL REPOSITORY OF THE MAGICIAN ARTHUR UNDERWOOD; CONCEALING IT SO THAT HE CANNOT OBSERVE IT.

THEN YOU ARE TO RETURN TO ME IMMEDIATELY TO AWAIT FURTHER INSTRUCTIONS.

VERY WELL. WHERE DOES THIS UNFORTUNATE MAGICIAN RESIDE?

DOWNSTAIRS.

OUCH.

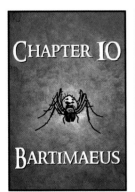

CHAPTER 10

BARTIMAEUS

DOWNSTAIRS? NOW THAT IS NASTY.

I JUST WANT IT SAFE. NO ONE'LL FIND IT THERE.

BUT IF THEY DO, YOU'RE IN THE CLEAR. TYPICAL MAGICIAN'S TRICK.

NO ONE'S GOING TO FIND IT.

YOU THINK NOT. WE'LL SEE.

FRAMING ANOTHER MAGICIAN WASN'T UNUSUAL.

MAGICIANS ARE THE MOST CONNIVING, JEALOUS, DUPLICITOUS GROUP OF PEOPLE ON EARTH, EVEN INCLUDING LAWYERS.

FRAMING YOUR OWN MASTER, THOUGH, NOW THAT *WAS* OUT OF THE ORDINARY.

I ENCASED THE AMULET WITH A CHARM, GIVING IT THE APPEARANCE OF A DRIFTING COBWEB.

THEN, IN SPIDER GUISE, I CRAWLED CAUTIOUSLY DOWN THROUGH THE CRACKS IN THE HOUSE.

AFTER SEVERAL MINUTES OF SCUTTLING, I FOUND THE STUDY.

THE SIMPLE TRAP AT THE ENTRANCE MIGHT HAVE SEEN OFF A CURIOUS HOUSEMAID, BUT NOT BARTIMAEUS.

THE AMULET DID ITS JOB AND ABSORBED THE BLAST.

IF THE BOY THOUGHT THE AMULET WOULD BE SAFE BEHIND HIS MASTER'S "SECURITY," HE HAD ANOTHER THINK COMING.

A PITIFUL ARRAY OF MAGICAL GIMCRACKS HAD BEEN ARRANGED HERE WITH SADLY LOVING CARE.

I ALMOST FELT SORRY FOR THE UNSUSPECTING DUFFER AS I PULLED THE COBWEB OVER A FAKE LUCKY RABBIT'S FOOT.

I WAS HEADING UP TO THE ATTIC ROOM AGAIN... WHEN THINGS GOT RATHER INTERESTING.

THE BOY WAS HEADING DOWNSTAIRS, TRAILING IN THE WAKE OF THE MAGICIAN'S WIFE.

HE LOOKED THOROUGHLY FED UP.

THIS WAS BAD. HE HAD LOST CONTROL OF THE SITUATION, A DANGEROUS THING FOR ANY MAGICIAN.

HE'S IN THERE. GO STRAIGHT IN...

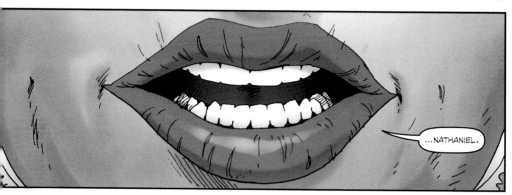

...NATHANIEL.

THE SPIDER REMAINED MOTIONLESS, BUT INWARDLY IT WAS THRILLED.

I HAD HIS NAME!

IN THE ROOM, I MADE IT EASY FOR *NATHANIEL* TO SPOT ME BY WIGGLING MY ABDOMEN IN A CHEERY FASHION.

I SEE MAKEPEACE IS FILLING THE THEATERS AGAIN WITH HIS EASTERN PIFFLE, *SWANS OF ARABY.*

I ASK YOU, SENTIMENTAL CLAPTRAP. HAVE YOU EVER SEEN A DJINNI WITH "EYES THAT WOULD MELT YOUR HEART"? MELT YOUR FACE, MAYBE.

ACTUALLY, I WAS RATHER HOPING TO GO.

HE SAW ME SCUTTLING AND WAVING AND WENT RATHER PALE.

FOUR MORE THEFTS IN THE LAST WEEK, MARTHA. *FOUR* MORE. AND VALUABLE ITEMS, TOO. I TELL YOU, WE'RE GOING TO THE DOGS.

AND THIS COFFEE IS COLD.

I'LL GET SOME MORE, DEAR.

SO YOU'RE HERE, ARE YOU?

YES, SIR. YOU SENT FOR ME, SIR.

I DID INDEED. NOW, I HAVE BEEN SPEAKING TO YOUR TEACHERS, AND WITH THE EXCEPTION OF MR. SINDRA, ALL HAVE SATISFACTORY REPORTS TO MAKE ON YOU.

HEAVEN KNOWS YOU DON'T DESERVE IT AFTER WHAT YOU DID LAST YEAR. HOWEVER...

I FEEL THE TIME IS RIGHT FOR YOU TO CONDUCT YOUR FIRST SUMMONS.

NATHANIEL, AS I WAS NOW DELIGHTED TO CALL HIM, WAS DISTRACTED. HE HAD A SPIDER ON HIS MIND.

ARE YOU LISTENING TO ME, BOY?!

IF YOU FRET AT THIS, YOU WILL NEVER MAKE A MAGICIAN OF YOURSELF. A WELL-PREPARED MAGICIAN FEARS NOTHING.

YES, SIR. OF COURSE, SIR.

I SHALL BE WITH YOU AT ALL TIMES IN THE CIRCLE AND WE WILL HAVE A DOZEN PROTECTIVE CHARMS TO HAND. PERHAPS WE SHALL START BY CAREFULLY SUMMONING A NATTERJACK IMPLING.

NATTERJACK IMPLING. SLIGHTLY LESS DANGEROUS THAN A PIECE OF MOLDY BREAD.

THE OTHER ARRANGEMENT WE NEED TO MAKE IS--

WAS THAT THE FRONT DOOR, SIR?

HOW DARE YOU INTERRUPT ME, BOY!

THE OTHER ARRANGEMENT, WHICH I SHALL WITHHOLD IF YOU ARE INSOLENT AGAIN, IS THE CHOOSING OF YOUR OFFICIAL NAME. WE SHALL TURN OUR ATTENTION TO THAT THIS AFTERNOON.

YES, SIR.

NATHANIEL WASN'T JUST HIS OFFICIAL NAME! IT WAS HIS REAL NAME!

THE FOOL HAD SUMMONED ME BEFORE CONSIGNING HIS BIRTH NAME TO OBLIVION. AND NOW I KNEW IT!

GET ON YOUR WAY, BOY.

I HAD A CHANCE WITH HIM NOW.

HE KNEW MY NAME AND I KNEW HIS.

HE HAD SIX YEARS' EXPERIENCE, I HAD FIVE THOUSAND AND TEN. THOSE WERE THE KIND OF ODDS YOU COULD DO SOMETHING WITH.

I WAS RACING AHEAD, EAGER FOR THE CONTEST TO BEGIN.

OH, THE BOOTS WERE ON THE OTHER EIGHT FEET NOW, ALL RIGHT.

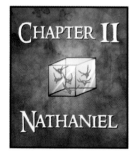

CHAPTER II

NATHANIEL

BEFORE.

THE DAY EVERYTHING CHANGED.

"Quickly, Nathaniel. The master wants to present you."

THIS IS THE BOY.

DO YOU BEAT HIM?

RARELY.

I'LL BET HE EATS LIKE A FERRET, TOO.

GREEDY, IS HE?

YES, SOME BOYS ARE.

LET'S SEE WHAT YOU'VE TAUGHT THIS WHIPPET OF YOURS, SHALL WE, UNDERWOOD?

IT'LL BE AMUSING.

HOW MANY CLASSIFIED TYPES OF SPIRIT ARE THERE?

THIRTEEN THOUSAND AND FORTY-SIX, SIR.

AND UNCLASSIFIED?

PETRONIUS POSTULATES FORTY-FIVE THOUSAND, SIR.

WHAT IS THE MODUS OPERANDI OF THE CARTHAGINIAN SUBGROUP?

THEY APPEAR AS CRYING INFANTS, SIR.

WHAT ARE THE SIX WORDS OF DIRECTION? ANY LANGUAGE.

APPARE; MANE; AUSCULTA; SE DEDE; PARE; REDI: APPEAR; REMAIN; LISTEN; SUBMIT; OBEY; RETURN.

BE FAIR, SIMON. HE CAN'T KNOW THAT YET!

BRAVO.

STANDARDS MUST HAVE DROPPED IF A BACKWARD APPRENTICE CAN BE CONGRATULATED FOR SPOUTING SOMETHING WE ALL LEARNED AT OUR MOTHERS' TEATS.

YOU'RE...

...YOU'RE JUST A SORE LOSER.

YOU COCKSURE GUTTERSNIPE. YOU'RE HELPLESS. YOU KNOW A FEW WORDS, BUT YOU'RE CAPABLE OF NOTHING.

GET OUT OF MY SIGHT.

LEAVE US, BOY.

"You're helpless."

"You're capable of nothing."

"You're helpless."

"You're capable of nothing."

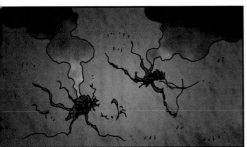

It is a long, wet autumn.

CHAPTER 12

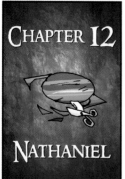

NATHANIEL

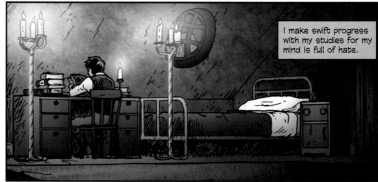

I make swift progress with my studies for my mind is full of hate.

GLADSTONE DID MORE THAN ANYONE ELSE TO HELP LONDON ASCEND TO MAGICAL PROMINENCE. SOON, LONDON OVERTOOK PRAGUE, WHICH HAD BECOME OLD AND DECADENT.

BY THEN ITS AILING MAGICIANS DID LITTLE BUT BICKER AMONG THE SLUMS OF THE OLD GHETTO.

ARE YOU LISTENING, LAD?

DO YOU KNOW WHAT THE IMPORTANT FACTS ARE HERE?

OH YES, SIR.

JUNIOR MINISTER FOR TRADE EYES CZECH DEAL

"I know what's important."

I steal an old piece of bronze sheeting from my master.

LEAVE US, BOY.

My "master" who did nothing to help me.

My real work starts here.

The humiliation of Simon Lovelace.

Dry-mouthed, I speak the words to summon and imprison the imp.

By applying certain persuasions, the imp can be induced to reveal true glimpses of things that are happening far away.

WHAT ARE YOU DOING? I'VE GIVEN YOU THE COMMAND, NOW OBEY!

TROUBLE IS, THIS ONE'S A BIT TRICKY, INNIT? HE'S GOT ALL SORTS OF MAGICAL BARRIERS UP.

I HOPE YOU REALIZE I'M ATTEMPTING THE NEAR-IMPOSSIBLE HERE TO GET PAST HIS DEFEN--

SHUT UP AND DO IT.

"Lovelace..."

OH IT'S HIM, ALL RIGHT. AND IF WE GET AWAY WITHOUT HIM SPOTTING US, WE'LL HAVE DONE WELL.

NOW, WHO IS THAT IN THE BLACK? AND WHERE DID HE SUDDENLY SPRING FROM?

NOW.

I CHARGE YOU TO--

NATHANIEL, EH? VERY POSH. DOESN'T REALLY SUIT YOU.

THAT'S NOT MY TRUE NAME.

I KNEW IT WAS GOING TO BE A DECENT SCRAP, AND I FIGURED WHAT WOULD ANNOY HIM MOST WAS TO APPEAR AS ANOTHER BOY OF ABOUT THE SAME AGE.

HE CAME OUT FIGHTING THOUGH, I'LL GIVE HIM THAT.

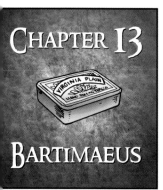

CHAPTER 13

VIRGINIA PLAIN

BARTIMAEUS

AS I HOPED, HE FORGOT HIMSELF AND WENT FOR THE OBVIOUS ATTACK.

NATHANIEL.

AND USING HIS BIRTH NAME I SENT IT STRAIGHT BACK AT HIM.

ZZZKKKK-KKKK

ZZZKKKKK-KKKKK

CAREFUL. NEARLY TOOK YOUR OWN HEAD OFF.

I KNOW A WAY YOU'LL STILL OBEY ME.

THE MOMENT YOU'VE GONE ON YOUR NEXT TASK, I SHALL CAST A SPELL OF INDEFINITE CONFINEMENT, BINDING YOU INTO THIS TIN.

UNFORTUNATELY FOR ME, HE WAS AN UNUSUALLY CLEVER AND RESOURCEFUL CHILD.

I have broken the cardinal rule.

The demon knows my birth name.

Panic wells up in my throat.

The cardinal rule... if you break that, you give yourself up for lost. Demons always find a way.

CHAPTER 14

NATHANIEL

No. I have only to work the confinement spell and everything will be fine.

I clasp my hands together to stop them shaking.

"Demons are very, very wicked. They will hurt you if they can."

"I'm worried about the boy. He barely touched his sandwich."

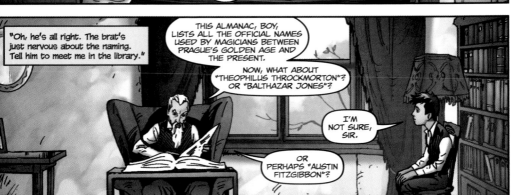

"The first stage of your education is complete... John Mandrake."

signature: John Mandrake

"I shall get this stamped at the ministry directly and you will then officially exist."

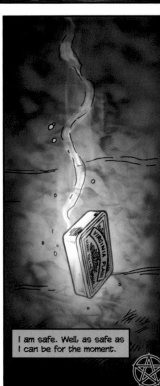

WHEN I FLEW OUT OF THE BOY'S ATTIC WINDOW, MY HEAD WAS SO FULL OF PLANS AND STRATAGEMS THAT I FLEW STRAIGHT INTO A CHIMNEY. THAT'S WHAT FAKE FREEDOM DOES FOR YOU.

OFF I WENT, ONE OF A MILLION PIGEONS IN THE GREAT METROPOLIS. BUT MY FREEDOM WAS AN ILLUSION.

MY YOUNG MASTER HAD MADE IT QUITE CLEAR WHAT WOULD HAPPEN IF I FAILED TO CARRY OUT MY MISSION TO SPY ON SIMON LOVELACE.

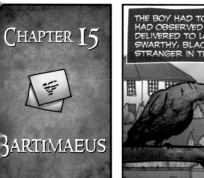

CHAPTER 15

BARTIMAEUS

THE BOY HAD TOLD ME HOW HE HAD OBSERVED THE AMULET BEING DELIVERED TO LOVELACE BY A SWARTHY, BLACK-BEARDED STRANGER IN THE DEAD OF NIGHT.

THE AMULET HAD EVIDENTLY BEEN STOLEN. ALL THE BOY WANTED WAS FOR ME TO FIND OUT THE DETAILS SO HE COULD EXPOSE AND HUMILIATE LOVELACE.

THAT WAS ALL.

I STARTED BY HEADING BACK TO WATCH LOVELACE'S PLACE. I WAS BOUND TO HAVE TO WAIT FOR AN HOUR OR SO.

THREE DAYS I WAITED.

THREE WHOLE DAYS.

EVERY EVENING, SEARCH SPHERES LEFT TO HUNT FOR THE AMULET. EVERY DAWN THEY RETURNED.

MORE OMINOUSLY, UNSPEAKABLE THINGS PROWLED AROUND THE GROUNDS INSIDE.

MY ONLY COMPANY WAS A LOVESICK PIGEON.

IT WAS TEMPTING TO TURN INTO AN ALLEY CAT. BUT THAT WOULD BE TOO RISKY.

ON THE MORNING OF THE THIRD DAY, SOMETHING HAPPENED AT LAST.

A MESSENGER IMP LEFT LOVELACE'S COMPOUND.

SOME SOCIETIES I HAD KNOWN MADE GREAT USE OF MESSENGER IMPS.

THE ROOFTOPS AND DATE PALMS OF OLD BAGHDAD USED TO SWARM WITH THE THINGS AFTER BREAKFAST AND SHORTLY BEFORE SUNDOWN.

I FOLLOWED AT A DISCREET DISTANCE AND WHEN WE WERE IN A REMOTE AREA I CHANGED AGAIN...

AND SWOOPED DOWN ON THE UNLUCKY IMP.

WHACKKKKK!

FIRST, I'M GOING TO READ THE LETTERS YOU'RE CARRYING. THEN I'M GOING TO ASK YOU SOME QUESTIONS ABOUT SIMON LOVELACE. OKAY?

YOU CAN STICK YOUR QUESTIONS UP YOUR—

THIS REPLACES A SHORT, CENSORED EPISODE CHARACTERIZED BY BAD LANGUAGE AND SOME SADLY NECESSARY VIOLENCE. WHEN WE PICK UP THE STORY AGAIN EVERYTHING IS AS BEFORE, EXCEPT THAT I AM PERSPIRING SLIGHTLY AND THE CONTRITE IMP IS THE MODEL OF COOPERATION.

HERE ARE THE LETTERS, O MOST BOUNTEOUS AND MERCIFUL ONE. ONE IS TO RUPERT DEVEREAUX, THE PRIME MINISTER.

THE OTHER I AM UNDER ORDERS TO DELIVER TO THE RESIDENCE OF MR. SCHYLER IN GREENWICH.

PINN'S ACCOUTREMENTS LOOKED LIKE A PALACE THAT HAD BEEN DROPPED ONTO THE STREET BY A GANG OF KNACKERED DJINN.

I GOT THERE JUST IN TIME TO SEE AN IMMENSELY FAT MAN PUT A "CLOSED" SIGN ON THE DOOR AND HAIL A CAB.

I TOOK THIS TO BE SHOLTO PINN HIMSELF.

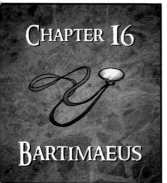

CHAPTER 16

BARTIMAEUS

I KNOCKED ANYWAY. LOUDLY. THE BOY WHO ANSWERED...

MESSAGE HERE FOR MR. SHOLTO FROM SIMON LOVELACE.

HE'S OUT. COME BACK LATER.

...WAS REALLY A FOLIOT ON THE SECOND PLANE.

DON'T WORRY, I'LL WAIT.

I'M NOT SUPPOSED TO LET ANYONE IN...HEY.

WOW. NOT MANY PEOPLE GET TO WORK IN A PLACE THIS POSH.

YOU'RE CERTAINLY RIGHT THERE.

STILL, I BET YOU PROBABLY GET STUCK WITH ALL THE HEAVY LIFTING AND CLEANING, EH?

YOU CHEEKY FUNGUS! THE MASTER VALUES ME MORE THAN THAT. I AM HIS ASSISTANT!

I KNEW THEN THAT I WAS DEALING WITH A COLLABORATOR OF THE WORST KIND.

I ENGAGED HIM WITH SICKENING FLATTERY FOR SEVERAL MINUTES BEFORE GETTING DOWN TO BUSINESS.

YOU HAD ANYTHING FAMOUS IN HERE, THEN?

THE HIGHLIGHT OF LAST YEAR WAS NEFERTITI'S ANKLE BRACELET. THAT WAS A SENSATION!

ALL A BIT OVER MY HEAD, GUV'NOR. I'LL TELL YOU SOMETHING I'VE HEARD OF... THAT AMULET OF SAMARAD THING?

YOU MEAN THE AMULET OF SAMARKAND, AND THERE YOU SHOW YOUR IGNORANCE.

"The Amulet was the property of the British Government until it was stolen six months ago. We would never handle stolen property."

"And there was a murder, too. Grisly and horrible. Not one alarm or magical trap was triggered. But there was poor old Mr. Beecham lying beside its empty case in a pool of blood...and the Amulet was gone."

THAT'S TERRIBLE, GUV'NOR, A MOST TERRIBLE THING.

I LOOKED AS MOURNFUL AS AN IMP COULD, BUT INSIDE I WAS CROWING WITH TRIUMPH.

SO LOVELACE HADN'T ONLY NICKED THE AMULET, HE'D HAD MURDER COMMITTED TO GET IT.

AND ON TOP OF THAT, HE'D STOLEN IT FROM HIS OWN GOVERNMENT... AND THAT WAS TREASON.

WELL, IF THIS DIDN'T PLEASE THE KID THEN I WAS A MONKFISH.

THAT AMULET MUST BE QUITE SOMETHING. USEFUL PIECE, IS IT?

IT IS SAID TO CONTAIN A MOST POWERFUL BEING.

"Something from the deepest areas of the Other Place, where chaos rules.

"The Amulet is claimed to protect the wearer against any attack by---"

THE FOLIOT BROKE OFF WITH A SUDDEN GASP...

-GULP-

I FIRED OFF A DETONATION.

KA-BOOM!

FPPPHEW!

BUT PINN HAD A PROTECTIVE FIELD AROUND HIM.

WACKKK!

I FIRED ANOTHER.

AS THE WINDOW BROKE, IT TRIGGERED A TRAP...

GLICHH!

SHHHSSSH!

WHOOOOSH!

MORE THAN ANYTHING, I FELT SORRY FOR THE DJINN ENSLAVED INSIDE THE MANNEQUINS.

WACKK!

CRASHHHHHHHH!

TIME TO QUIT WHILE I WAS AHEAD.

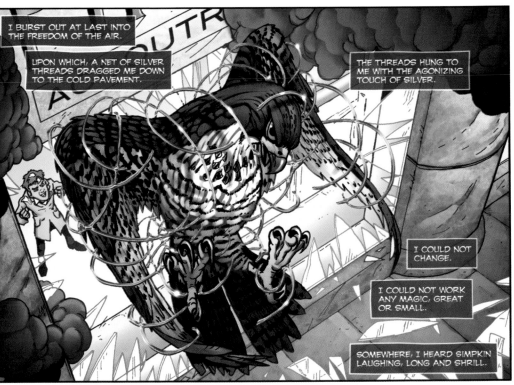

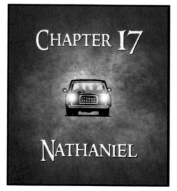

Chapter 17

Nathaniel

Several hours to go and I'm already dressed in my best clothes.

YOU'RE READY EARLY. THAT HONEY AND LEMON HAS CLEARLY GOT YOU BACK ON YOUR FEET..."JOHN."

My new name sounds strange. Fake.

It's been three days since my magical duel with Bartimaeus and my trip to the Thames. Most of them spent in bed with a bad head cold.

WHO WILL BE THERE TONIGHT...AT PARLIAMENT?

YOU KNOW VERY WELL. THE THREE HUNDRED MINISTERS OF THE GOVERNMENT, THEIR HUSBANDS AND WIVES, A FEW HANGERS-ON, AND SOME VERY LUCKY NAMED APPRENTICES... LIKE YOU, JOHN.

NOW I HAVE TO GET READY, OR I'LL BE LATE MYSELF.

Parliament.

SIT IN THE BACK, BOY, AND DO NOT TOUCH THE WINDOWS.

Seeing the city up close takes my breath away.

THAT'S ONE, MARTHA! ONE OF THE WORST PUBS. I'D SEND THE NIGHT POLICE IN TOMORROW IF IT WERE UP TO ME.

OH, NOT THE NIGHT POLICE, ARTHUR. THERE MUST BE BETTER WAYS OF REEDUCATING THEM.

SHOW ME A LONDON PUB, MARTHA, AND I'LL SHOW YOU A COMMONERS' MEETING HOUSE HIDDEN INSIDE. FILTHY DIVES AND PITS LIKE THAT ARE WHERE ALL THIS RESISTANCE TROUBLE IS STARTING.

Silent onlookers stand on the sidewalks watching the procession of cars. Their faces are sullen, even hostile.

Most of them look thin and drawn and cold.

I have a name. I am on my way to Parliament.

A Government vigilance sphere hangs in the air and relays the scene to hidden eyes. We join the queue of the great and the good to go inside.

I have arrived.

I CAN'T WAIT TO SEE IF CAFTANS ARE STILL IN THIS YEAR.

MARTHA, PLEASE.

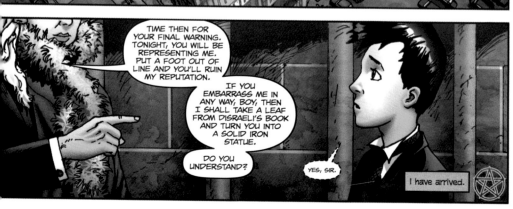

TIME THEN FOR YOUR FINAL WARNING. TONIGHT, YOU WILL BE REPRESENTING ME. PUT A FOOT OUT OF LINE AND YOU'LL RUIN MY REPUTATION.

IF YOU EMBARRASS ME IN ANY WAY, BOY, THEN I SHALL TAKE A LEAF FROM DISRAELI'S BOOK AND TURN YOU INTO A SOLID IRON STATUE.

DO YOU UNDERSTAND?

YES, SIR.

I have arrived.

Chapter 18

Nathaniel

I DO LOVE TO WATCH THE FAMOUS ONES... SUCH A PLEASURE.

"That's Mr. Duvall, the Chief of Police. I met him once, John—what a charming man."

SHOULDN'T WE... YOU KNOW... TALK TO SOMEONE?

I THOUGHT I TOLD YOU TO KEEP QUIET, BOY.

"That's Maurice Schyler. He's something in the Government. I don't know what."

OH, AND THAT'S QUENTIN MAKEPEACE, THE PRIME MINISTER'S FAVORITE PLAYWRIGHT.

"Don't tell Mr. Underwood, but I think he's rather marvelous. His plays are so romantic."

"Jessica Whitwell, she's something to do with Security. Caught those Czech infiltrators ten years ago."

"Good heavens!"

"That's the merchant, Sholto Pinn.

"Whatever happened to him? Poor soul."

I feel suddenly reduced to insignificance. The unrated apprentice of an unrated magician.

AND OF COURSE YOU KNOW ...FROM THAT RATHER UNFORTUNATE INCIDENT LAST YEAR.

"That's the Junior Minister for Trade—Simon Lovelace."

An uncomfortable prickling breaks out in my stomach. The feeling of weakness annoys me.

LADIES AND GENTLEMEN, MY NAME IS QUENTIN MAKEPEACE, AND AS MOST OF YOU KNOW, I'M NO STRANGER TO THE STAGE MYSELF.

There's nothing to fear. Lovelace has no way of tracing the Amulet to me.

I am safe enough. And I should seize this opportunity like any good magician.

TONIGHT, IT'S MY GREAT PLEASURE TO INTRODUCE MY DEAR FRIEND RUPERT DEVEREAUX. LADIES AND GENTLEMEN, OUR PRIME MINISTER!

I sidle through the crowd while everyone is distracted.

THANK YOU, THANK YOU. GIVING A STATE ADDRESS IS A PARTICULARLY PLEASANT TASK FOR ME; REQUIRING AS IT DOES THAT I BE SURROUNDED BY SO MANY WONDERFUL PEOPLE...

HERE WE GO. MORE FLANNEL FROM THE OLD CHARMER.

NEVER MIND HIM. I'VE HAD NO LUCK WHATSOEVER... NOTHING I'VE SUMMONED CAN TELL ME WHO CONTROLS IT.

TONIGHT, I'M PLEASED TO BE ABLE TO REPORT SUCCESS ON ALL FRONTS, BOTH AT HOME AND ABROAD.

YOU'RE WASTING YOUR TIME. HOW WOULD THE OTHER DEMONS KNOW?

I stay in the shadows and strain to hear their voices.

NEGOTIATIONS IN THE AMERICAN COLONIES GO WELL, AND CLOSER TO OUR SHORES, OUR ARMIES HAVE FOUGHT THE ITALIAN REBELS TO A STALEMATE NEAR TURIN.

YOU GOT MY MESSAGE? I THINK WE SHOULD CANCEL.

CANCEL?

CHAPTER 19
NATHANIEL

The sphere shatters and the elementals trapped inside recoil from each other with ferocious and savage force.

Air, earth, fire, and water.

People are blown backwards.

Pelted with rocks.

Lacerated with fire.

And deluged with water.

The crowd is sent sprawling like skittles.

Night Police swarm over the river terrace.

The Prime Minister has already gone, whisked away to safety by a powerful afrit.

Most of the crowd weren't so lucky.

I find Mrs. Underwood and feel a little teary with relief.

ARE YOU ALL RIGHT?

YES. I THINK SO. BUT WHERE'S ARTHUR?

I spot him looking rather dazed.

ANYONE SEE WHAT HAPPENED?

IT HAPPENED TOO FAST.

SOME OBJECT, THROWN FROM BEHIND.

PERHAPS A RENEGADE MAGICIAN USING A PORTAL? OR THE RESISTANCE?

EXCUSE ME, SIR. I SAW HIM...

BY HEAVENS, BOY, IF YOU'RE LYING...

NO, SIR. HE HAD A BLUE ORB.

IT WAS AN ELEMENTAL SPHERE, I'M SURE. HE RAN IN FROM THE TERRACE AND THREW IT.

IT HAS TO BE THE RESISTANCE. UNDERWOOD, INTERNAL AFFAIRS IS YOUR DEPARTMENT. HAVE ANY ELEMENTAL SPHERES BEEN STOLEN?

I CAN'T SAY. CONFIDENTIAL INFORMATION.

DON'T MUTTER INTO WHAT'S LEFT OF YOUR BEARD, MAN. WE'VE A RIGHT TO KNOW.

LADIES, GENTLEMEN, LET'S NOT BULLY POOR ARTHUR NOW.

ARTHUR ISN'T RESPONSIBLE FOR THIS OUTRAGE, POOR FELLOW.

YOU SAW THE ATTACKER DID YOU, YOUNG UNDERWOOD? AS YOU ARE HERE THIS EVENING, I TAKE IT YOU NOW HAVE YOUR NAME?

YES, SIR. JOHN MANDRAKE, SIR.

SHARP AS EVER I SEE, JOHN. YOU'RE TO BE CONGRATULATED; NO ONE ELSE GOT SO MUCH AS A LOOK AT HIM.

I'M SURE THAT THE POLICE WILL WANT A STATEMENT FROM YOU BEFORE YOU LEAVE. SEE THEY GET IT.

YES, SIR.

WE MUST BE GRATEFUL THAT THE PRIME MINISTER IS SAFE AND THAT NO ONE IMPORTANT WAS HURT.

MIGHT I HUMBLY SUGGEST THAT YOU ALL HEAD HOME TO RECUPERATE—AND PERHAPS TREAT YOURSELVES TO A CHANGE OF CLOTHES.

OF ALL THE ARROGANT—

YOU WOULDN'T THINK HE WAS ONLY A JUNIOR MINISTER.

COME WITH ME, BOY.

ALL I CAN HOPE IS THAT WHAT HAPPENED TONIGHT WILL ENCOURAGE THEM TO GIVE ME MORE FUNDS.

IF THEY DON'T, WHAT CAN THEY EXPECT? WITH A MEASLY DEPARTMENT OF SIX MAGICIANS, I'M NOT A MIRACLE WORKER!

I DON'T THINK ANYONE IS BLAMING YOU FOR THE THEFTS, DEAR.

NO, BUT THEY WILL SOON.

WE'RE HOME.

MARK MY WORDS— AFTER TONIGHT, ANYONE CAUGHT IN POSSESSION OF STOLEN MAGICAL PROPERTY WILL SUFFER THE MOST SEVERE PENALTY.

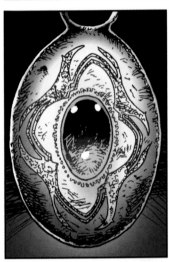

THEY WON'T DIE EASILY, YOU CAN BE SURE OF THAT.

SLAM

HOT CHOCOLATE BEFORE BED, DEAR?

CHAPTER 20

BARTIMAEUS

WHEN THE DARKNESS CLOAKING MY MIND LIFTED, I FOUND MY FALCON FORM HAD DETERIORATED...

I HAD BECOME A THICK, OILY VAPOR SLOSHING BACK AND FORTH IN MIDAIR.

IT WAS ABOUT THE NEAREST I EVER GOT TO REVEALING MY PURE ESSENCE.

I QUICKLY CHANGED MYSELF INTO A SLENDER HUMAN FEMALE AND LOOKED AROUND...

I WAS TRAPPED INSIDE AN ENERGY SPHERE OF CONSIDERABLE POWER. JUST TOUCHING IT WOULD CAUSE ME UNBEARABLE PAIN.

THERE WAS NO OPENING. NO WEAK SPOT. NO ESCAPE.

I WAS IN BIG TROUBLE.

HELLO THERE. THAT'S A VERY FINE TOASTING FORK.

SPEAK OUT OF TURN AND I'LL PRICK YOU FULL OF HOLES.

THE GUARDS WERE TWO SIZABLE UTUKKU—A TYPE OF DJINNI FAVORED FOR THEIR UNINTELLIGENT DEVOTION TO VIOLENCE.

I ONCE SLAUGHTERED AN INFEASIBLE NUMBER OF UTUKKU AT THE INFAMOUS BATTLE OF AL-ARISH WITH THE OLD "HE'S BEHIND YOU" TRICK.

MY COLLEAGUE THINKS HE KNOWS YOU.

I'VE SMELT YOU FOR CERTAIN, LONG TIME AGO.

GREAT. SURVIVORS OF THE BATTLE. I TRIED TO CHANGE THE SUBJECT...

I ASSUME I'M IN THE HANDS OF THE GOVERNMENT? BUT WHERE, EXACTLY?

"You're in the Tower of London..."

"AND THAT'S GOOD, IS IT?"

"Not for you."

I DO. I KNOW YOU...

FRIEND OF A FRIEND MAYBE?

NO... AN ENEMY, I THINK.

TERRIBLE WHEN YOU CAN'T REMEMBER SOMETHING THAT'S RIGHT ON THE TIP OF YOUR TONGUE, ISN'T IT? AND SOME FOOL IS PRATTLING AWAY, DISTRACTING YOU AND...

SHUT UP! I NEARLY HAD IT THEN.

A TREMOR RAN THROUGH THE ROOM AND TWO FIGURES STEPPED OUT OF THIN AIR. IF YOU'RE ME, THIS HAPPENS A LOT.

WELL, IT'S AWAKE NOW. LET'S SEE WHAT IT HAS TO SAY.

WE WANT YOUR NAME AND YOUR PURPOSE IN ATTACKING MR. PINN'S SHOP. AND MOST OF ALL, WE WANT THE NAME OF YOUR MASTER.

PINN'S FACE LOOKED AS THOUGH AN ELEPHANT HAD JUST GOTTEN UP FROM IT. I ALLOWED MYSELF A SMILE.

GO ON, GIVE ME A WINK BACK...

IT'S GOOD EXERCISE FOR A BRUISED EYE.

YOU ARE NOT IN A POSITION TO BE IMPUDENT, DEMON. LET ME CLARIFY THE SITUATION FOR YOU.

"This is the Tower of London, where all enemies of the Government are brought for punishment.

"No creature has ever left here, save at our pleasure.

"This chamber is protected by three layers of hexlocks.

"Between each layer are vigilant battalions of horlas and utukku, patrolling constantly."

YOU ARE IN A MOURNFUL ORB.

TOUCH IT, AND IT WILL TEAR YOUR VERY ESSENCE.

THE ORB WILL GRADUALLY SHRINK. YOU CAN SHRINK TOO, I'M SURE, BUT THE ORB CAN SHRINK TO NOTHING—AND THAT YOU CANNOT DO.

ENOUGH OF THIS, JESSICA. REDUCE THE ORB.

MR. PINN IS HERE BECAUSE HE WISHES TO SEE YOUR PAIN.

AND IF I DO TALK, WHAT HAPPENS TO ME THEN?

IF YOU COOPERATE, WE'LL LET YOU GO. WE HAVE NO INTEREST IN KILLING SLAVES.

"Well?"

SHE SOUNDED SO BRUTALLY FORTHRIGHT, I ALMOST BELIEVED HER. BUT NOT QUITE.

I COULD HAVE TAKEN A GAMBLE AND DROPPED THE KID RIGHT IN IT, BUT:
1) THEY WOULD PROBABLY KILL ME ANYWAY.
2) IT WAS QUITE POSSIBLE THAT PINN WAS IN LEAGUE WITH LOVELACE. (THEY HAD BEEN HAVING LUNCH TOGETHER, REMEMBER?)

I WAS ABOUT TO GIVE THEM A FINAL TIRADE OF ABUSE WHEN...

...I FELT A FAMILIAR SENSATION. I WAS BEING SUMMONED!

I WOULD SOON BE FREE.

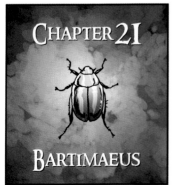

CHAPTER 21

BARTIMAEUS

A SUMMONING—NOW I COULD DISAPPEAR FROM UNDER THEIR ANNOYING NOSES.

SO SORRY, I'D LOVE TO HELP YOU, REALLY I WOULD. BUT I HAVE TO GO. MAYBE WE CAN PICK UP THE TORTURE AND CAPTIVITY AGAIN SOMETIME SOON. SO LONG...

THE PAIN OF THE SUMMONING WAS WORSE THAN NORMAL.

SHARPER...LESS HEALTHY.

AFTER TWO DEEPLY UNPLEASANT MINUTES...

...THE VICIOUS TUG OF THE SUMMONS DIED AWAY.

THAT WAS WORTH THE PRICE OF ADMISSION ON ITS OWN, DEAR JESSICA.

IT IS IMPOSSIBLE TO LEAVE A MOURNFUL ORB, AND THAT INCLUDES BY SUMMONING. EVEN YOUR MASTER CANNOT CALL YOU FROM IT.

SHE'LL FIND A WAY.

"SHE"? YOUR MASTER IS A WOMAN?

IT LIES. AN OBVIOUS BLUFF. I AM WEARY AND I SHOULD BE IN THE STEAM ROOM AT THE BYZANTINE BATHS. THE ORB CONTRACTS EVEN NOW. MIGHT I SUGGEST WE LEAVE THE CREATURE TO IT?

AN ADMIRABLE IDEA.

FASCINATING...IN A TIME OF CRISIS, IT BECOMES A DESERT CAT. VERY EGYPTIAN. THIS ONE'S HAD A LONG CAREER, I THINK.

THE ORB WILL CONTINUE TO SHRINK. IF YOU CHANGE YOUR MIND AND WISH TO AVOID DEATH, THEN TELL THE GUARDS HERE.

OVER THE NEXT FEW HOURS, MY SITUATION GREW EVER LESS COMFORTABLE.

JUST TO ADD TO MY PAIN, THE BOY TRIED TO SUMMON ME TWICE MORE.

WERE YOU AT THE SIEGE OF ANGKOR THOM?

NO, I WASN'T. LOOK, YOU'RE OBVIOUSLY A CLEVER FELLOW. IF YOU LET ME OUT OF HERE, I'LL KILL YOUR MASTER AND SET YOU FREE.

YOU MUST THINK I'M STUPID.

NO, THAT'S WHAT *HE* SAID.

WHAT?

STOP TALKING TO THE PRISONER, YOU IDIOT.

IDIOT, AM I?

YEAH.

YEAH?

YEAH?

BARTIMAEUS!

WHAT?!?

I KNOW YOU NOW! YOUR VOICE...IT IS YOU— THE DESTROYER OF MY PEOPLE! AT LAST! I HAVE WAITED TWENTY-SEVEN CENTURIES FOR THIS MOMENT!

WHEN YOU'RE FACED WITH A COMMENT LIKE THAT, IT'S HARD TO THINK OF ANYTHING TO SAY.

NNYYAAARRRGHHHH!

I SETTLED FOR WHIRRING MY WINGS. YOU KNOW, IN A FORLORN, DEFIANT SORT OF WAY.

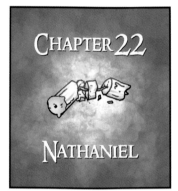

CHAPTER 22

NATHANIEL

The worst day of my life starts as it means to go on.

"Mark my words, after tonight, anyone caught in possession of stolen magical property will suffer the most severe penalty."

What had started as a personal strike against my enemy suddenly now seems a far riskier business.

I need to get rid of the Amulet fast. Return it to Lovelace and then alert the authorities in some way.

Three times I perform a summons and three times Bartimaeus does not appear.

No time to clean up now.

Perhaps there are other methods of summoning in my Master's library.

Yes, the library is the place I should...

WELL, I HOPE YOU'RE SATISFIED WITH YOURSELF. FROM WHAT ARTHUR TELLS ME, YOU HAVE BEEN VERY BAD INDEED.

Mrs. Underwood's words are full of quiet disappointment. I feel tears prick the corners of my eyes.

OH NATH--JOHN. WHY COULDN'T YOU WAIT? MS. LUTYENS USED TO SAY IMPATIENCE WAS YOUR ABIDING FAULT. AND SHE WAS RIGHT.

MR. UNDERWOOD SAID MY CAREER IS RUINED.

I SHOULDN'T BE SURPRISED IF IT WERE...

MRS. UNDERWOOD!

PERHAPS IF YOU ARE HONEST AND OPEN WITH THE MASTER ABOUT WHAT YOU'VE DONE; THEN THERE'S A CHANCE HE WILL LISTEN TO YOU. AND PERHAPS EVEN FORGIVE YOU IN TIME.

HE WON'T. HE'S TOO ANGRY.

I WILL DO MY BEST TO APPEASE HIM, TOO.

"Mr. Underwood was only coming upstairs to tell you that your summoning practice this afternoon would have to be delayed.

"He's had to go into work. Some emergency. A rogue djinni has been caught at Pinn's in central London.

"At least *that's* not your fault."

CHAPTER 23

BARTIMAEUS

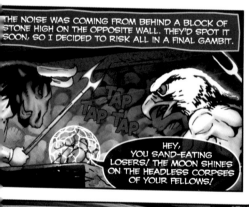

AN ENORMOUS BLACK RAVEN SWOOPED DOWN, FOLLOWED BY ANOTHER ONE.

THERE WAS A BLUR OF MOVEMENT, A SNAP, AND TWO GULPS.

THEN THE TWO UTUKKU WERE GONE.

EVEN I DON'T SEE *THAT* EVERY DAY.

ONE OF THE RAVENS GAVE A SHIMMY AND TOOK ON AN ALL-TOO-FAMILIAR GUISE...

OH. HELLO.

HELLO, BARTIMAEUS.

CHAPTER 24

BARTIMAEUS

AND JABOR, TOO. HOW NICE OF YOU BOTH TO COME.

WE THOUGHT YOU MIGHT BE LONELY, BARTIMAEUS.

NOW, TELL US WHERE YOU SECRETED THE AMULET OF SAMARKAND AND IF YOU SPEAK RAPIDLY, WE MIGHT HAVE TIME TO DESTROY THE ORB BEFORE YOU PERISH.

REVERSE THAT SEQUENCE AND YOU COULD HAVE YOURSELVES A DEAL.

WE BOTH KNOW THAT IF I TELL YOU THE LOCATION, YOU'LL LEAVE ME TO DIE. THEREFORE, I'LL OBVIOUSLY GIVE YOU FALSE INFORMATION JUST TO SPITE YOU. SO ANYTHING I SAY FROM IN HERE WILL BE WORTHLESS. AND THAT MEANS YOU'VE GOT TO LET ME OUT.

ANNOYING, BUT I SEE YOUR POINT.

THE KINDLY MAGICIANS WHO PUT ME IN HERE MENTIONED LEGIONS OF HORLAS AND UTUKKU—I SHOULD THINK THAT'S THEM ARRIVING NOW... I DOUBT EVEN JABOR CAN SWALLOW THEM ALL.

SO PERHAPS WE COULD CONTINUE THIS DISCUSSION A LITTLE LATER?

AGREED.

PALE-FACED HORLAS FOUGHT TO GET OUT OF THE PORTAL, HOLDING THEIR LITTLE TRIDENTS AND SILVER NETS IN THEIR STICK-THIN ARMS.

IT WAS TIME TO GO.

CCCCKKKKKKKKKKKKKKKKKKKKKKK!

(FROM A POCKET IN HIS COAT, AQUARL PRODUCED A RING OF IRON SOLDERED TO A METAL ROD. WELL, HE WOULDN'T WANT TO TOUCH THE IRON—UGH!)

MARVELOUS. IF ONLY WE'D HAD A DRUM ROLL.

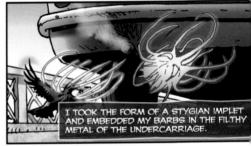

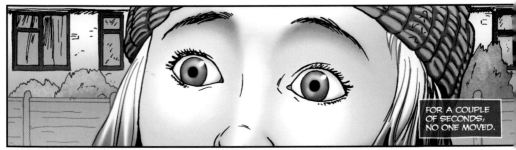

FOR A COUPLE OF SECONDS, NO ONE MOVED.

YOU SMELL OF PETROL.

FAQUARL BEGAN A GESTURE. I SENSED HIS REGRETFUL INTENTION.

WHY DID I ACT THEN? PURE SELF-INTEREST. BECAUSE WITH FAQUARL MOMENTARILY DISTRACTED, IT WAS THE PERFECT OPPORTUNITY TO ESCAPE.

AND IF I HAPPENED TO SAVE THE GIRL TOO... WELL, IT WAS ONLY FAIR. IT WAS SHE WHO GAVE ME THE IDEA, AFTER ALL.

DON'T YOU...

WHHHHOOOSH!

EEEEEEEEEEEEEKKK!

IN A MOMENT, I WAS IN THE AIR AND HURTLING AT TOP SPEED TOWARD MY STUPID, MISBEGOTTEN MASTER.

Dusk.

The scrying disk shows me nothing useful.

The magical defenses at the Tower mean my imp can't even get close.

Mrs. Underwood brings up a tray.

WHAT... WHAT'S HAPPENING? IS THE MASTER HOME?

HE'S RETURNED AND LOCKED HIMSELF IN HIS STUDY. THERE'S QUITE AN EMERGENCY ON.

In that instant, I decide to tell her everything. She is the only person who cares.

MRS. UNDERWOOD?

NOT NOW, JOHN. I HAVEN'T TIME.

BUT I REALLY NEED TO--

NOT A WORD MORE. I HAVE TO GO.

The door shuts. The key turns.

The urge to cry turns quickly to anger.

I am not a naughty child to be left moping in the attic.

I am a magician.

MY MASTER IS IN HIS STUDY. GO CLOSE, SO I CAN SEE AND HEAR EVERYTHING.

WHO'S A LITTLE SNEAK, THEN? SORRY, YOUR MORALS AREN'T MY BUSINESS. WELL, HOLD ON TIGHT. HERE WE GO...

He speaks a word. The imp's viewpoint freezes.

Moments later, my bedroom door bursts open.

TRAITOR! YOU HAVE BETRAYED ME! WHO IS GUIDING YOU TO SPY ON YOUR OWN MASTER?

NO ONE— THERE'S NO ONE.

MISERABLE BOY! TELL ME, WHO IS CONTROLLING YOU? WHICH OF MY ENEMIES? DUVALL? MORTENSEN? OR PERHAPS LOVELACE?

NONE OF THOSE, SIR. THERE IS NO ONE.

LIAR! WE WILL GO TO MY STUDY, WHERE YOU WILL ENJOY THE COMPANY OF MY MANY IMPS UNTIL YOUR TONGUE IS LOOSENED. COME!

KNOCK! KNOCK!

KNOCK! KNOCK! KNOCK!

I'M COMING. I'M COMING.

OH.

GOOD EVENING, MRS. UNDERWOOD.

YOUR HUSBAND HAS BORROWED A LITTLE SOMETHING OF MINE.

AND I'M RATHER KEEN TO GET IT BACK.

CHAPTER 26

NATHANIEL

Mrs. Underwood calls upstairs to say that Simon Lovelace has arrived. My master immediately throws me into the box room.

TYPICAL OF LOVELACE TO TURN UP AT THE WORST POSSIBLE MOMENT.

SIR, PLEASE LISTEN. IT'S IMPORTANT. IN YOUR STUDY...

SILENCE!

SIR!

I hear him turn the key and then his footsteps on the stairs.

I am alone in the dark.

SIR! SIR!!

SIR!

ACTUALLY, I FIND "SIR" A BIT FORMAL FOR MY TASTE, BUT IT'S BETTER THAN "RECREANT DEMON."

BARTIMAEUS! YOU BROUGHT LOVELACE HERE! HE'S DOWNSTAIRS RIGHT NOW. YOU'VE BETRAYED ME!

ME? I'VE SAID NOTHING. I'VE GOT THAT TOBACCO TIN TO THINK OF...

IT IS A SLIGHT COINCIDENCE THOUGH, I MUST ADMIT.

"SLIGHT"? YOU'VE LED HIM HERE, YOU FOOL!

GO TO THE STUDY QUICKLY, AND GET THE AMULET OUT OF THE HOUSE BEFORE LOVELACE FINDS IT.

NOT A CHANCE. HE'LL HAVE A DOZEN SPHERES AND SERVANTS STATIONED OUTSIDE THE HOUSE.

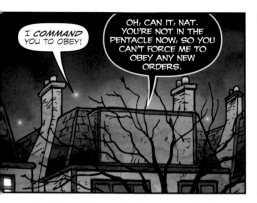

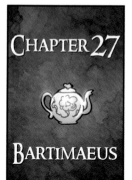

CHAPTER 27

BARTIMAEUS

BY THE TIME MY SPIDER FORM CRAWLED DISCREETLY OVER THE LINTEL, LOVELACE WAS ALREADY APPLYING THE THUMBSCREWS.

YOU SEEM FLUSTERED, UNDERWOOD.

I WAS ENGAGED AT THE TOP OF THE HOUSE. I AM SOMEWHAT OUT OF BREATH.

THE BOY'S FUTURE—AND CONSEQUENTLY MINE—DEPENDED ON MY REACTING QUICKLY TO WHATEVER HAPPENED NOW.

A FEW NIGHTS AGO, I SUFFERED A THEFT. AN ITEM OF SOME POWER WAS STOLEN FROM MY HOUSE.

AND YOU THINK THE RESISTANCE WAS RESPONSIBLE?

ACTUALLY, I DON'T. I SUSPECT THE THEFT WAS THE WORK OF A FELLOW MAGICIAN.

HOW CAN YOU BE SURE?

BECAUSE I KNOW WHAT CARRIED OUT THE RAID. IT WAS A MID-RANKING DJINNI OF GREAT IMPUDENCE AND SMALL INTELLIGENCE, NAMED BARTIMAEUS.

AT THIS POINT, SOMEONE WITH EXCELLENT HEARING MIGHT HAVE HEARD A SPURT OF WEBBING BEING SHOT FURIOUSLY INTO THE CEILING IN A CORNER OF THE ROOM.

AS TO WHO SUMMONED IT... WELL, ARTHUR, THAT IS WHY I AM HERE. TO SEE YOU.

LOVELACE CHOSE HIS WORDS WITH CARE. ON HIS SHOULDER, HIS SECOND-PLANE IMP SAT WATCHING THE OLD MAN.

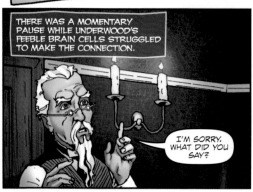

THERE WAS A MOMENTARY PAUSE WHILE UNDERWOOD'S FEEBLE BRAIN CELLS STRUGGLED TO MAKE THE CONNECTION.

I'M SORRY. WHAT DID YOU SAY?

THE DJINNI IN QUESTION LATER ATTACKED PINN'S OF PICCADILLY, AND WAS CAPTURED AND IMPRISONED IN THE TOWER.

IT ESCAPED THIS AFTERNOON AND WAS FOLLOWED BY MY AGENTS. FOLLOWED ALL THE WAY... BACK HERE.

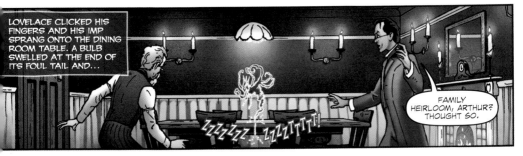

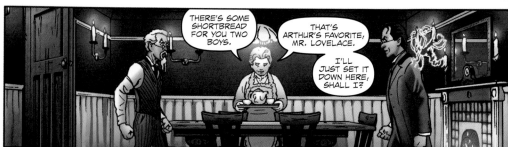

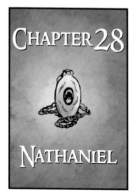

Chapter 28

Nathaniel

Panic rushes through my head.

Slowly, steadily, over the last few days, everything has spiraled out of my control.

I hear Mrs. Underwood gently humming as she hurries around downstairs.

Mrs. Underwood... who I have placed in terrible danger.

Running and hiding are the advice of a treacherous demon. Not the actions of an honorable magician.

I know what I must do.

I arrive just in time to witness the moment of discovery.

HA! WELL, WELL, WHAT HAVE WE HERE?

NO... IT'S A TRICK... YOU'RE FRAMING ME. I DON'T KNOW HOW THAT GOT THERE...

HE'S TELLING THE TRUTH. *I* TOOK IT.

THE PERSON THAT YOU WANT IS ME.

WHAT ARE YOU GIBBERING ABOUT, YOU FOOL? GET OUT!

A MOMENT, ARTHUR. PERHAPS YOU'RE BEING TOO HASTY.

DON'T BE ABSURD! THIS STRIPLING CANNOT HAVE COMMITTED THE CRIME. HE WOULD HAVE NEEDED TO BYPASS BOTH OUR DEFENSES...

"Not to mention being able to summon a most powerful and sophisticated djinni.

"Oh."

BUT WHY WOULD YOU STEAL ANYTHING FROM ME?

I do not think my master has recognized what the Amulet really is. And that may yet save him.

IT WAS JUST A TRICK, SIR. A JOKE. I WANTED TO GET BACK AT YOU FOR HITTING ME THE TIME I RELEASED THE MITES.

THIS IS THE LAST STRAW, BOY! I WILL HAVE YOU UP BEFORE THE COURTS FOR THIS.

WE HAVE BOTH BEEN INCONVENIENCED, LOVELACE. HE HAS BETRAYED ME, AND FROM YOU HE HAS STOLEN THIS VALUABLE AMULET...

My master fell silent.

In that sudden, fatal instant, he realized what the Amulet was.

AND...AND WE SHALL BOTH SEE HIM SUITABLY PUNISHED, YES WE WILL. AND HE'LL REGRET THE DAY HE STOLE THE...ERR... THING.

My master went to speak again, but Lovelace raised a hand to bid him be quiet.

WELL, JOHN MANDRAKE, I AM *ALMOST* IMPRESSED. TO SUMMON A DJINNI SUCH AS BARTIMAEUS AT YOUR AGE IS NO MEAN FEAT.

YOU LEFT ME FRUSTRATED, WHICH IS A RARE EVENT, AND UNDERWOOD IGNORANT, WHICH IS SOMEWHAT LESS UNUSUAL.

ONE THING PUZZLES ME. WHAT POSSESSED YOU TO OWN UP TO YOUR ACTIONS NOW?

BECAUSE IT WASN'T MY MASTER'S FAULT. HE KNEW NOTHING. YOUR QUARREL WAS WITH ME, WHETHER YOU KNEW IT OR NOT.

SOME CHILDISH CONCEPT OF NOBILITY, IS IT? HEROIC, BUT STUPID.

AS YOU HAVE SEEN, SIMON, I AM ENTIRELY INNOCENT IN THIS AFFAIR. DO WHAT YOU WANT WITH THE BOY. LEAVE ME ALONE.

SUCH LOYALTY FROM A MASTER TO HIS APPRENTICE! A FINAL LESSON IN THE ART OF BEING A MAGICIAN, JOHN. WE HAVE NO HONOR, NO NOBILITY, NO JUSTICE.

IT MAY CONSOLE YOU TO KNOW THAT EVEN BEFORE YOU ARRIVED, I WAS RESOLVED TO KILL YOU AND EVERYONE IN THIS HOUSE. I CANNOT LEAVE ANYTHING TO CHANCE.

YOUR STUPIDITY IN COMING HERE AND CONFESSING HAS CHANGED NOTHING.

Tears flood my eyes.

PLEASE— MRS. UNDERWOOD IS DOWNSTAIRS.

YOU ARE WEAK, BOY, LIKE YOUR MASTER.

He makes a sign. Something terrible materializes in the corner of the room.

YOUR WISH?

DESTROY THEM BOTH, AND ANYTHING ELSE LIVING IN THE HOUSE. BURN IT TO THE GROUND WITH ALL ITS CONTENTS.

Before I can scream, claws seize me around the throat.

CHAPTER 29

BARTIMAEUS

I GIVE UNDERWOOD'S DESK THE CREDIT.

IT WAS AN OLD-FASHIONED, STURDY AFFAIR.

CRRRRRACCCCKKKK!

IN THE SECONDS IT TOOK JABOR TO SMASH IT, I BECAME A GARGOYLE, GRABBED MY YOUNG MASTER, AND RAN.

WE WENT ALMOST UNNOTICED.

UNDERWOOD SENT A BOLT OF BLUE FIRE CRACKING TOWARD LOVELACE...

BUT THE AMULET OF SAMARKAND ABSORBED THE ENTIRE ATTACK.

WE'D JUST GOT PAST THE MAIN LANDING...

WHEN WE HEARD UNDERWOOD'S SCREAM.

A MOMENT LATER...

A COLOSSAL EXPLOSION RIPPED THROUGH THE HOUSE.

AN OVERZEALOUS ATTACK, AND QUITE TYPICAL OF JABOR.

MRS. UNDERWOOD?

KA-BOOM!

THE DETONATION FLEW PAST AND EXPLODED HARMLESSLY. (TO ME, WHICH IS WHAT COUNTS.)

KA-KEEEEE

KA-KEEEEE

EVERY TIME JABOR FIRED, THE FORCE OF HIS SHOTS WEAKENED THE ROOF.

BUT I WAS TIRING.

I HIT THE ROOF HARD.

MY RETURN SHOT WAS WEAK AND LOW. IT STRUCK THE ROOF AT JABOR'S FEET.

HE LET OUT A TRIUMPHANT LAUGH, WHICH WAS CUT SHORT...

...BY THE ROOF COLLAPSING.

NOOOOOO!

CRRRR-AACCCCK!

THERE WAS NO SIGN OF ANY OF LOVELACE'S OTHER SLAVES. NO DJINN, NO WATCHFUL SPHERES.

PERHAPS, WITH THE AMULET BACK IN HIS HANDS, HE HAD NO NEED OF THEM.

I SUMMONED UP MY REMAINING STRENGTH AND WE SLUNK AWAY INTO THE NIGHT.

BEHIND US, THE WAIL OF FIRE ENGINES SOUNDED IN THE STREET...

...AND ANOTHER GREAT BEAM CAME CRASHING DOWN INTO THE FLAMING RUINS OF HIS MASTER'S HOUSE.

WE QUIETLY DISAPPEARED INTO THE DARK.

Dawn. And I'm still too tired to sleep.

We spent most of the night running.

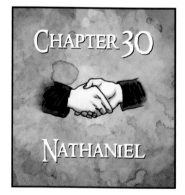

CHAPTER 30

NATHANIEL

BRITISH MUSEUM
TREASURES
OF THE
EMPIRE
EXHIBITION

WORLD

F. ELLIOT
FAMILY
BUTCHER

NEWS

FORREST

WHAT WAS THIS PLACE, DO YOU THINK? A LIBRARY?

DON'T SUPPOSE THE COMMONERS ARE ENCOURAGED TO READ MUCH ANYMORE, ARE THEY? THAT'S USUALLY THE WAY IT GOES.

YOU'RE SHIVERING. BUT THEN I SUPPOSE YOU'RE HARDLY DRESSED FOR A WINTER EXPEDITION.

I COULD MAKE A FIRE. YOU ONLY HAVE TO ASK.

YES. MAKE A FIRE.

NOW *THAT* WASN'T VERY POLITE.

MAKE ME A FIRE, *PLEASE.*

MUCH BETTER.

YOU'RE AN INTERESTING SPECIMEN. I MEAN POPPING IN, UTTERLY DEFENSELESS, TO TELL A POWERFUL ENEMY THAT YOU PINCHED HIS TREASURE.

BE SILENT.

I HAD ANOTHER MASTER LIKE YOU ONCE. HE HAD THE SAME MULISH OBSTINACY, SELDOM ACTED IN HIS OWN BEST INTERESTS.

DIDN'T LIVE LONG.

SO WHAT NOW? YOU COULD FLEE TO PRAGUE. I HEAR THE BEER'S GOOD.

I'M NOT GOING TO SLINK AWAY. LOVELACE MURDERED MRS. UNDERWOOD, THE ONLY PERSON WHO EVER CARED FOR ME. I WANT JUSTICE FOR HER.

GIVE IT UP, NAT. LOOK AROUND YOU. YOU'VE LOST EVERYTHING A MAGICIAN NEEDS—WEALTH, SECURITY, SELF-RESPECT, A MASTER. YOU'VE GOT NOTHING.

I HAVE MY SCRYING GLASS. AND I HAVE YOU.

AH YES, I WAS COMING TO THAT. I'VE COMPLETED MY CHARGE. AND MORE. IT'S TIME TO SET ME FREE.

NOT YET.

CHAPTER 31

NATHANIEL

First we need to know what the authorities are saying about last night.

YOU LOOK ROUGH, CHUM. BEEN OUT ALL NIGHT?

CERTAINLY NOT.

The paperboy suddenly looks at my coat with an intense interest.

I KNOW A PLACE IF YOU GOT ANYTHING TO SELL.

THANK YOU...ERR... I HAVEN'T.

THAT WAS STRANGE.

JUST GO AND GET THE STUFF.

Bartimaeus steals me food and clothes. He isn't long returning.

THEY'RE SAYING I STARTED THE FIRE. THAT I KILLED THEM.

WHAT DID YOU EXPECT?

SO WHAT ARE WE ACTUALLY GOING TO DO, O GREAT MASTER?

WHEN I WAS AT THE RECEPTION AT PARLIAMENT, I HEARD PEOPLE TALKING ABOUT A CONFERENCE LOVELACE WAS ORGANIZING OUT OF TOWN.

SNEAKILY DONE. I HEARD THE SAME THING FROM LOVELACE HIMSELF. I THINK HE'S USING THE AMULET IN SOME PLAN TO SEIZE POWER. *THAT* OLD STORY.

HE'S A RENEGADE, A BACK-STABBING TRAITOR!

YEP, HE'S A MAGICIAN, ALL RIGHT.

I SHALL ATTEND THE CONFERENCE MYSELF AND EXPOSE THE PLOT THERE. FIRST WE NEED TO FIND OUT WHERE AND WHEN IT'S TAKING PLACE.

IF ONLY I HAD MY BOOKS, SOME PROPER INCENSE, AND A SELECTION OF CANDLES, I COULD SEND OUT AN ARMY OF IMP SPIES TO GET THE INFORMATION.

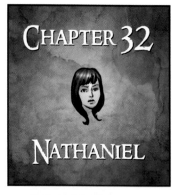

I wake in the dark.

Dusk has fallen.

Bartimaeus has still not returned and the fire is dead.

EVENING EDITION!

Another newspaper might be useful.

Bartimaeus told me to stay inside, but I do not care to be told what to do by demons.

YOU STILL OUT ON THE STREET?

EVENING EDITION, PLEASE.

I'VE JUST SOLD OUT. BUT LUCKY FOR YOU, MY MATE WILL HAVE SOME LEFT.

COME ON, WE'LL GO ROUND TO THE NAG'S HEAD. I ALWAYS MEET HIM THERE AT THE END OF THE DAY. HE'LL HAVE A PAPER FOR YOU.

HELLO, FRED. I'VE BROUGHT A CHUM TO SEE YOU.

HE'S THE ONE I WAS TELLING YOU ABOUT. HE'S GOT IT ON HIM NOW.

WELL? HAVE YOU GOT A PAPER?

NO. I'VE RUN OUT, TOO.

I should never have come down here. I turn to leave.

HOLD ON, CHUM.

WE'RE NOT TRYING TO ROB YOU. WE'RE JUST INTERESTED IN WHAT YOU'VE GOT IN YOUR COAT.

THERE'S NOTHING IN MY COAT.

STANLEY KNOWS, DON'T YOU, STANLEY?

WE JUST WANT TO SEE WHAT YOU'VE STOLEN, THAT'S ALL. DON'T WORRY. WE'RE NOT COPS OR MAGICIANS.

I wish Bartimaeus were here.

MODERN PIECE. VERY CRUDELY DONE. HOMEMADE, I'D SAY. NOTHING SPECIAL, BUT WORTH HAVING.

My heart speeds up. Is this the Resistance in action? I think fast.

I WAS UP IN HIGHGATE. BIG POSH HOUSE, OPEN WINDOW. TOO GOOD TO MISS. I THOUGHT MAYBE I COULD SELL IT.

YEAH? WELL, YOUR LUCK'S IN. COME WITH US AND WE'LL ARRANGE A MEETING.

I CAN'T COME NOW.

SHAME.

My scrying disk disappears inside the boy's coat.

HEY! GIVE ME THAT B--OOOF!

WACKKKK.

Fury overcomes dizziness and I set off in unsteady pursuit.

UHHHHHH

I strain to hear their words and edge nearer.

CLINK!

WHHAAGGGK!?

SHALL I CUT HIS THROAT FOR YOU, KITTY?

NO... HE'S ONLY A STUPID KID. LET'S GO.

HAD A GOOD EVENING, SIR?

DID LOVELACE FIND YOU? DID JABOR BREAK IN?

I WENT OUT FOR A NEWSPAPER.

CHAPTER 33

BARTIMAEUS

MY MASTER SPUN ME A SAD STORY ABOUT BEING ROBBED BY TWO NEWSPAPER BOYS AND A GIRL.

...THEN THEY TOOK MY SCRYING DISK AND IT WAS ONLY THE GIRL THAT STOPPED THEM FROM KILLING ME. ONE DAY I'LL FIND THEM AND MAKE THEM PAY.

DID YOU LOCATE HEDDLEHAM HALL?

OF COURSE.

MY MASTER WANTED TO SET OFF FOR THE HALL IMMEDIATELY, BUT DON'T IMAGINE THAT STOPPED HIM FROM COMPLAINING...

AND THEN IT TOOK ME HOURS TO FIND MY WAY BACK TO THE BUILDING *AND I HURT MY KNEE.* AND WHY DO WE HAVE TO GO THIS HORRIBLE WAY? IT'S ALL MUD.

WE'RE GOING THIS WAY BECAUSE THERE IS A CURFEW ON AND SEARCH SPHERES IN THE STREETS. AND BECAUSE, SADLY, I NEED TO GET YOU TO THE RAILWAY STATION ALIVE.

IT WAS STRANGE, THE PAPERBOY JUST SEEMED TO KNOW I HAD THE DISK WITHOUT EVEN SEEING IT. LIKE HE WAS A DJINNI OR AN IMP.

INTERESTING...

THEY SOUNDED EXACTLY LIKE THE BUNCH OF KIDS WHO'D JUMPED ME THE NIGHT I STOLE THE AMULET.

IF THEY WERE PART OF THIS RESISTANCE MOVEMENT, IT SEEMED THE OPPOSITION TO THE MAGICIANS WAS MORE FORMIDABLE THAN I'D THOUGHT.

I DIDN'T SHARE THESE THOUGHTS WITH THE BOY. HE WAS THE ENEMY, AFTER ALL.

"THERE...THAT'S HEDDLEHAM HALL. I SHOULD TELL YOU THAT THE PLACE IS SURROUNDED BY THE MOST FORMIDABLE DEFENSES I'VE SEEN SINCE I BROKE INTO SOLOMON'S PALACE.

"AIRBORNE FOLIOTS PATROL THE SKIES."

"THERE ARE AT LEAST TWO PROTECTIVE DOMES OVER THE ESTATE ITSELF.

"HIGH-RANKING ENTITIES MATERIALIZE AT RANDOM ACROSS THE GROUNDS."

AND WORSE, I CAN FEEL IN MY ESSENCE THAT THEY'RE HIDING SOMETHING IN THERE. SOMETHING VERY UNPLEASANT.

A SOUND DREW OUR FOCUS BACK TO THE ROAD. A MAGICIAN'S BLACK CAR ROARED ALONG.

IT TURNED THE CORNER AND HEADED TOWARD THE HOUSE, THEN IT CAME TO A STOP AT THE GATE. THE SENTRIES HUNG BACK WHILE A HUMAN FIGURE APPROACHED IT.

A FEW MOMENTS LATER, AND THE LITTLE CAR WAS CONTINUING ON TOWARD THE HALL.

WELL, AT LEAST THAT TELLS US WHAT WE HAVE TO DO.

I FELT A TERRIBLE SENSE OF UNEASE.

WE SETTLED IN FOR THE NIGHT.

MY MASTER SLEPT, OR TRIED TO. I TOOK THE GUISE OF A BAT.

THE CLOUD COVER DRIFTED AWAY AND THE STARS SHONE DOWN.

I WONDERED IF LOVELACE WAS READING THEIR IMPORT FROM THE ROOF OF THE HALL.

CHAPTER 34

SQUALLS & SON

BARTIMAEUS

BY THE TIME DAWN ARRIVED, MY MASTER APPEARED TO HAVE CAUGHT A CHILL.

ACHOO!

YOU SHOULD HAVE ASKED ME FOR A FIRE.

I'M NOT ILL.

THE BOY GULPED DOWN THE LAST OF THE STOLEN FOOD

THE CROSSROADS WERE THE PLACE FOR THE AMBUSH. ANY APPROACHING VEHICLES HAD TO SLOW DOWN HERE FOR FEAR OF AN ACCIDENT. AND A THICK CLUMP OF TREES CONCEALED IT FROM THE GATEWAY.

THE FIRST CAR THAT PASSED WAS TRAVELING IN THE WRONG DIRECTION. IT CAME FROM THE HOUSE.

AND ANYWAY, IT WAS A MAGICIAN'S CONVERTIBLE, NO DOUBT CONTAINING ONE OF THE CONSPIRATORS.

THE NEXT THREE VEHICLES WERE ALL HEADING THE RIGHT WAY, BUT WERE ALSO MAGICIAN'S CARS.

NEXT, HUFFING AND PUFFING, CAME A BUTCHER'S BOY ON HIS BICYCLE. HE WAS NO GOOD TO US EITHER.

ABOUT AN HOUR LATER, A GROCER'S VAN APPEARED.

SQUALLS AND SON.

PERFECT.

MY NEW FIELD MOUSE GUISE SHOT INTO THE AIR, AND IN THROUGH THE OPEN WINDOW OF THE VAN.

NEITHER SQUALLS NOR SON HAD TIME TO REACT.

SQUALLS & SON

THE VAN ROCKED VIOLENTLY TO AND FRO AS I TOOK CARE OF BUSINESS.

A MAN WHO LOOKED LIKE SQUALLS GOT OUT OF THE VAN, REACHED BACK IN, AND STARTED TO PULL OUT THE UNCONSCIOUS FORMS OF SQUALLS AND SON.

WE'LL HIDE THEM IN THE HEDGE. GET THE KID'S CLOTHES AND PUT THEM ON. HURRY.

FAQUARL WOULD HAVE ARGUED SIMPLY TO DEVOUR OUR VICTIMS, WHILE JABOR WOULDN'T HAVE ARGUED AT ALL, BUT JUST SCOFFED THEM. BUT I FIND THAT THE GRIME OF HUMAN FLESH IS RATHER LIKE EATING BAD SEAFOOD. UGH.

SENTRIES RACED ACROSS THE FIELD AS I STRUGGLED TO GET THE VAN MOVING AGAIN.

GET CHANGED, QUICK AS YOU CAN.

AS WE DROVE, THE BOY HAD THE BRIEFEST OF GLANCES IN THE BACK TO SEE WHAT WE WERE CARRYING.

THE ENTRANCE TO THE HEDDLEHAM HALL ESTATE CAME INTO SIGHT WITH ITS GREAT ARCH AND GATEWAY.

WHY ARE YOU SHIVERING?

IT'S HIM... THE ONE I SAW IN MY SCRYING GLASS, THE ONE WHO BROUGHT THE AMULET TO LOVELACE.

SQUALLS & SON

STROLLING CASUALLY, SMILING A LITTLE SMILE, THE MURDERER APPROACHED THE VAN.

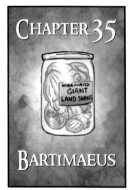

CHAPTER 35

BARTIMAEUS

SO HERE HE WAS—THE MAN WHO HAD STOLEN THE AMULET OF SAMARKAND AND VANISHED WITHOUT A TRACE.

SQUALLS AND SON?

THE MAN WHO HAD CUT ITS KEEPER'S THROAT AND LEFT HIM LYING IN HIS BLOOD.

LOVELACE'S HIRELING.

WHAT HAVE YOU BROUGHT?

GROCERIES, GUV'NOR.

NAMELY?

BOXES, TINS, PACKETS OF THINGS, BOTTLES, TINS, MORE TINS...

YOU DON'T SOUND VERY SPECIFIC.

A HIGH VOICE SOUNDED AT MY ELBOW.

THAT'S BECAUSE HE DIDN'T TAKE THE LIST, SIR. I DID.

WE'VE GOT BALTIC CAVIAR, PLOVERS' EGGS, FRESH ASPARAGUS, CURED BOLOGNESE SALAMI, SYRIAN OLIVES, LARKS' TONGUES IN ASPIC, GIANT LAND SNAILS MARINATED IN THEIR SHELLS, WIRRAL OYSTERS, OSTRICH MEAT—

THE HIRELING WANTED TO INSPECT THE GOODS FOR HIMSELF.

AS I OPENED THE REAR DOORS OF THE VAN, I DEVOUTLY WISHED THE BOY HAD NOT LET HIS IMAGINATION RUN AWAY WITH HIM.

VERY WELL.

YOU MAY CONTINUE TO THE HOUSE. IT IS THE PROPERTY OF A GREAT MAGICIAN. DO NOT STRAY OR TRESPASS IF YOU VALUE YOUR LIVES.

HOW DID YOU...?

I HAVE BEEN TRAINED. I READ FAST AND REMEMBER ACCURATELY.

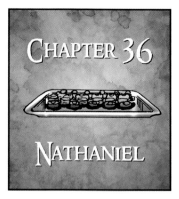

CHAPTER 36

NATHANIEL

I watch Lovelace smiling at his guests. Mrs. Underwood died because he stole the Amulet. Now I will destroy him.

I SAW THE ROOM FOR THE FIRST TIME ONLY THIS MORNING. SIMON SAID IT WOULD TAKE MY BREATH AWAY AND HE WAS RIGHT.

THE CARPET HAS TO BE SEEN TO BE BELIEVED!

THANK GOODNESS, FOOD! FAMISHING JOURNEY FROM LONDON.

ARE YOU SERVING THOSE, BOY, OR TAKING THEM FOR A WALK?

SORRY, SIR.

I pick up a new tray and loiter until there is a sudden stir in the crowd...

LADIES AND GENTLEMEN! OUR BELOVED PRIME MINISTER, RUPERT DEVEREAUX....

ON BEHALF OF LADY AMANDA AND MYSELF, SIR, MAY I WELCOME YOU TO HEDDLEHAM HALL.

THE SPEECHES WILL BEGIN SHORTLY IN THE GRAND SALON, WHICH LADY AMANDA HAS REFURBISHED ESPECIALLY FOR TODAY.

I'M LOOKING FORWARD TO IT, LOVELACE.

WOULD YOU EXCUSE ME, SIR? I MUST JUST COLLECT SOME PROPS FOR MY OPENING SPEECH. THEN WE'LL BE READY FOR THE BIG EVENT.

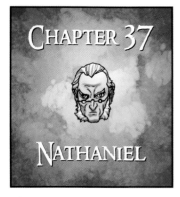

CHAPTER 37

NATHANIEL

Lovelace sneaks away... with me on his trail.

Now I am the one doing the hunting.

I am careful not to make the slightest noise.

SIMON? WHAT'S WRONG?

I'VE BROUGHT YOU A PRESENT... THE BOY.

COME HERE, CHILD.

HOW DID YOU KNOW I WAS HERE?

RUFUS LIME RECOGNIZED YOU.

HAVE YOU LOST YOUR DEMON, BOY? THAT IS A CARELESS THING.

DEVEREAUX ARRIVED WITH A FORMIDABLE AFRIT. DO YOU THINK HE SUSPECTS?

NO. NORMAL PARANOIA, SHARPENED BY THAT CURSED ATTACK ON PARLIAMENT.

ONCE IN POWER, WE MUST ROOT OUT THIS "RESISTANCE" AND HANG THE STUPID CHILDREN UP ON TOWER HILL.

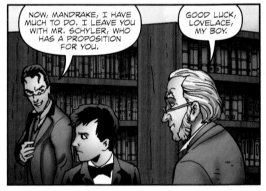

NOW, MANDRAKE, I HAVE MUCH TO DO. I LEAVE YOU WITH MR. SCHYLER, WHO HAS A PROPOSITION FOR YOU.

GOOD LUCK, LOVELACE, MY BOY.

SIMON WAS MY APPRENTICE BEFORE HE WAS YOUR AGE. I WAS FOR KILLING YOU STRAIGHT AWAY; BUT HE IS MORE FARSIGHTED.

DON'T BOTHER LOOKING AT THOSE TRINKETS FOR HELP. THEY'RE JUST WORTHLESS TOYS OF THE UNEDUCATED RICH.

IN A FEW MINUTES, LAD, THE HUNDRED MOST POWERFUL MINISTERS IN THE GOVERNMENT WILL BE DEAD, ALONG WITH OUR SAINTED P.M. WE WILL NEED TALENTED NEW MAGICIANS TO HELP US RULE THE COUNTRY.

JOIN WITH US, AND YOU CAN HAVE THE APPRENTICESHIP YOU HAVE ALWAYS CRAVED.

LET US DRAW OUT YOUR POWER SO THAT IT CAN FLOURISH...

Six years of suppressed desire—to be recognized for what I am...to exercise power...to go to Parliament as a great minister of State...

Six years of suppressed desire...

DOES SIMON LOVELACE *REALLY* THINK I WILL JOIN HIM? AFTER EVERYTHING THAT HAS HAPPENED?

HE DOES....

THEN HE'S A FOOL. AN ARROGANT FOOL.

AFTER WHAT HE HAS DONE TO ME, HE COULD OFFER UP THE WORLD AND I'D REFUSE. JOIN HIM? I WOULD RATHER DIE.

VERY WELL.

ORDINARILY, I WOULD ENJOY KILLING YOU SLOWLY...BUT SADLY, TODAY I CANNOT SPARE THE TIME.

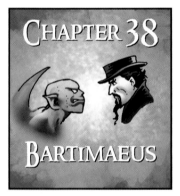

CHAPTER 38

BARTIMAEUS

I HOPED THE BOY COULD KEEP OUT OF TROUBLE LONG ENOUGH FOR ME TO REACH HIM.

GETTING IN WAS TAKING LONGER THAN I THOUGHT.

THE LIZARD SCUTTLED UP AND DOWN, BUT THE PLACE WAS TOO WELL-SEALED.

ONE WING OF THE HOUSE DREW MY ATTENTION. POWERFUL MAGICAL BARS CRISSCROSSED ALL THE WINDOWS AS FAR AS THE SEVENTH PLANE. BUT THEY WERE ON THE INSIDE...

MY CURIOSITY WAS PIQUED.

BEYOND WAS A VAST CIRCULAR HALL.

FROM WALL TO WALL IT GLINTED AND GLEAMED.

THE EXTRAORDINARY THING ABOUT THE ROOM WAS THE FLOOR. IT WAS MADE OF GLASS.

BENEATH THE GLASS STRETCHED AN IMMENSE AND VERY BEAUTIFUL CARPET. I WOULD HAVE BEEN RATHER IMPRESSED...

...HAD I NOT SPOTTED LOVELACE'S HORRID MUG THERE... AMONG OTHERS.

A FISH-FACED MAN ENTERED THE ROOM. HE CARRIED THE SUMMONING HORN THAT I HAD SEEN IN LOVELACE'S STUDY.

HMM... A SUMMONING HORN...

I BEGAN TO SEE DAYLIGHT. THE ROOM'S MAGICAL DEFENSES WEREN'T DESIGNED TO KEEP ANYTHING OUT. THEY WERE DESIGNED TO KEEP EVERYONE IN.

IT WAS DEFINITELY TIME I FOUND THE BOY AGAIN.

I CLIMBED HIGHER ONTO THE ROOF, AND AS I DID SO, SAW AN UNWELCOME SIGHT. THREE FIGURES WERE RACING TOWARD THE HOUSE.

MR. SQUALLS, FOR ONE, WAS MOVING ALONG AT A GOOD PACE FOR SOMEONE WHO HAD RECENTLY BEEN KNOCKED ABOUT BY A FIELD MOUSE.

THE BEARDED MERCENARY SEEMED TO MOVE WITH SUPERHUMAN SPEED.

HIS STRIDES SEEMED ORDINARY ONES, BUT THEY ATE UP THE GROUND AT BLINDING PACE.

THEN I SAW HE WAS WEARING SEVEN-LEAGUE BOOTS. SO *THAT'S* HOW HE *GOT AWAY* WITH STEALING THE AMULET.

SEVEN-LEAGUE BOOTS = A POTENT MAGICAL DEVICE. EACH BOOT CONTAINS A CAPTIVE DJINNI WHO CAN BEND TIME AND SPACE.

I CHANGED FORM AGAIN.

THIS WASN'T THE TIME TO BE DISCREET.

MY FIRST DETONATION VAPORIZED A SMALL HONEYSUCKLE BY THE LAKE.

MY SECOND CAUGHT THE MERCENARY IN THE CHEST.

HE DISAPPEARED IN A MASS OF SAPPHIRE FLAMES.

ONLY TO REAPPEAR—VERY MUCH ALIVE.

I DELIVERED ANOTHER, MORE CONCENTRATED BLAST...

...TO NO EFFECT.

NOW *THAT* WAS ANNOYING.

THE MAN TOOK A SILVER DISK FROM INSIDE HIS COAT AND THREW IT.

IT BIT INTO MY ARM, POISONING ME WITH SILVER.

THAT DID IT. I'D BEEN THROUGH A LOT IN THE LAST FEW DAYS.

I'D BEEN SUMMONED, MANHANDLED, SHOT AT, CAPTURED, THREATENED, AND GENERALLY TAKEN FOR GRANTED.

I LOST MY TEMPER.

THE ANGRIEST GARGOYLE YOU'VE EVER SEEN RIPPED THE STATUE FROM ITS FOUNDATIONS AND SMASHED IT DOWN ON THE MERCENARY.

TEDIOUSLY, HE WAS STILL ALIVE.

WELL, IF I COULDN'T STOP HIM, I COULD CERTAINLY SLOW HIM DOWN. I UNLACED HIS BOOTS...

...AND THREW THEM AS HARD AS I COULD INTO THE MIDDLE OF THE LAKE.

YOU'LL PAY FOR THAT.

SPLASH

THEN, SUDDENLY...

OUCH.

I FELT MY INSIDES BEING SUCKED OUT THROUGH MY BACK.

MY FORM GREW VAPOROUS AND WEAK.

STOP, COWARD!

I'M LETTING YOU OFF AND DON'T YOU...

THEN I WAS GONE, AND MY REBUKE WITH ME.

CHAPTER 39

NATHANIEL

KA-BOOM

I grab what I can from the display table and run.

Prague Cubes. Party gimmicks. Not weapons, but maybe useful.

I dodge from bookcase to bookcase.

THERE'S NOWHERE TO RUN, BOY.

KA-BOOM

P-FIZZzzzz

HOW CHARMING! MORE, PLEASE. I WISH TO SMELL MY VERY BEST WHEN WE TAKE OVER THE COUNTRY.

I move silently behind Schyler.

And throw three Prague Cubes at once.

P-BOOM!

They were a lime-green Catherine Wheel, a ricocheting Viennese Cannon, and an Ultramarine Bonfire.

CRRACCK

He hits the wall headfirst.

Maurice Schyler does not get up.

His neck is broken.

I draw the lines I need to summon Bartimaeus.

YOU REALLY HAVE GOT PERFECT TIMING, HAVEN'T YOU? I'D JUST GOT OLD BEARDY EXACTLY WHERE I WANTED HIM!

IT'S ABOUT TO START. WE NEED TO MOVE QUICKLY.

The gargoyle leaps through the house.

I THINK LOVELACE IS SUMMONING SOMETHING.

YOU DON'T SAY.

WE'RE TOO LATE.

THAT'S THE ROOM. QUICKLY, FLATTEN YOUR HAIR DOWN. YOU CAN ENTER AS A SERVANT. HURRY.

Bartimaeus changes into a new, much smaller form.

WHO ARE YOU?

THEY WANT SOMEONE EXTRA FOR THE DRINKS, SIR.

I can feel Bartimaeus as a small insect in my ear.

CLIICKKK

Behind us, the door swings shut. Locks click into position and huge bolts are drawn.

I'D LIKE TO WELCOME YOU ALL TO AN EXTRAORDINARY EVENT...

OH DEAR. NOW, THAT DOES SOUND OMINOUS.

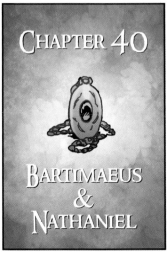

CHAPTER 40

BARTIMAEUS & NATHANIEL

"Firstly, I'd like to draw your attention to the carpet on display below. It was commissioned from Persia, just for today."

WE BELIEVE IT'S THE LARGEST SUCH CARPET IN THE COUNTRY. YOU SHOULD ALL FIND YOURSELVES IN IT IF YOU LOOK CAREFULLY.

"And now may I introduce your true host... The Right Honorable Simon Lovelace..."

CLAP CLAP CLAP

PRIME MINISTER, LADIES AND GENTLEMEN, MAY I SAY HOW HONORED WE ARE THAT YOU COULD JOIN US TODAY.

"THIS IS OUR LAST CHANCE. LOVELACE WILL SPRING HIS TRAP ANY MOMENT. GET DOWN THERE."

LOVELACE IS PLANNING SOMETHING! THIS IS A TRAP!

HOW DARE YOU DISRUPT THIS MEETING, BOY!

LOVELACE HAS GOT THE AMULET OF--

SILENCE, BRAT!

WHITWELL ENCLOSED THE BOY IN A STRICTURE. NO OBJECT OR NOISE COULD ESCAPE THE WEB OF THREADS.

A terrible helplessness floods over me.

"DON'T BOTHER SHOUTING. NO ONE CAN HEAR US. SHE'S SEALED US OFF."

I'LL LOOK FOR A WEAK LINK. ALL STRICTURES HAVE THEM SOMEWHERE.

We're right at the center of Lovelace's scheme.

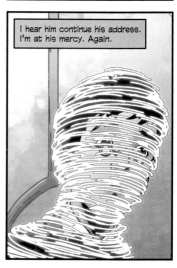

I hear him continue his address. I'm at his mercy. Again.

"ONE CRUMB OF COMFORT... IT CAN'T BE ANYTHING TOO POWERFUL, OR LOVELACE WOULD HAVE HAD TO USE A PENTACLE."

MAY I DRAW YOUR ATTENTION TO THE REMARKABLE CEILING, WITH ITS COLLECTION OF PRICELESS CHANDELIERS.

"They were taken from the ruins of Versailles after the French Wars."

Through the web of the Stricture, I am aware of the floor moving.

Something is covering the carpet.

No, the carpet's not being covered. It's being drawn back underneath the glass floor, quickly and stealthily.

No one notices. While the magicians gawk at the ceiling, the floor below them changes.

It is now a giant pentacle. And we are all inside.

"Erm...Bartimaeus..."

"WHAT? I'M TRYING TO CONCENTRATE AND FIND US A WAY OUT."

"The floor..."

"OH.

"THAT'S BAD."

AFTER THAT, EVENTS HAPPENED FAST.

LOVELACE RAISED THE HORN TO HIS LIPS AND BLEW. IT MADE NO SOUND IN THE ROOM, BUT IN THE OTHER PLACE IT WOULD HAVE RUNG LOUD.

THE MAGICIANS UNDERSTOOD NOW. THEY LAUNCHED ATTACKS IN LOVELACE'S DIRECTION, BUT THE AMULET DID ITS WORK.

LOVELACE JUST SMOOTHED BACK HIS HAIR AND SMILED.

SOME MAGICIANS TRIED THE DOORS WITHOUT SUCCESS.

DEVEREAUX'S AFRIT ATTEMPTED TO FLY HIM OUT OF ONE OF THE WINDOWS, BUT THE MAGIC SEALS HELD FIRM. THEY BOTH TUMBLED BACK TO EARTH.

I SAW A FLICKER IN THE AIR.

THEN SOMETHING TORE A HOLE IN THE REALITY OF THE WORLD AND STARTED TO PUSH ITS WAY THROUGH.

MY ESSENCE SHIVERED.

CHAPTER 41

BARTIMAEUS &
NATHANIEL

NATHANIEL, LISTEN TO ME. NEXT TIME ONE OF THOSE RIPPLES PASSES NEAR US, GET READY TO JUMP INTO IT. UNDERSTAND?

INTO IT?!

WHEN WE'RE FREE, WE NEED TO DO TWO THINGS. FIRST, GET THE AMULET FROM LOVELACE. THAT'S YOUR JOB. I'LL DISTRACT HIM, YOU GRAB IT.

SECOND, REVERSE THE SUMMONS AND DRIVE OUR BIG FRIEND AWAY. I'LL STEAL THE HORN, BUT YOU'LL HAVE TO FIND A MAGICIAN STRONG ENOUGH — AND ALIVE ENOUGH — TO PERFORM THE DISMISSAL SPELL.

"HERE COMES ANOTHER RIPPLE. YOU READY?

"JUMP!"

KA-PPPOOOM!

I stumble to my feet and move around behind Lovelace.

An ugly fly buzzes along the ground.

BZZZZZZT

BZZZZZZZZT

BZZZZZZZZZZT

BZZ—

Oh no.

Lovelace makes a sign, and a hulking shape with a jackal's head materializes at his shoulder.

SO, YOU REJECTED MY OFFER? A PITY. I PRESUME THIS "FLY" IS BARTIMAEUS.

JABOR, KILL BARTIMAEUS. DO NOT FAIL ME THIS TIME.

I CHANGED INTO A GARGOYLE AND DARTED INTO THE AIR.

ACROSS THE CHAOTIC HALL WE FLEW, AVOIDING THE HUMANS, EXPLOSIONS, AND SHOCK WAVES.

YOU KNOW, JOHN, IF YOU'D HAD THE LUCK TO BE APPRENTICED TO ME FROM THE START, WE MIGHT HAVE DONE GREAT THINGS TOGETHER.

WE SHARE THE SAME WILL TO POWER. EVEN NOW YOU HAVEN'T GIVEN UP.

AGGGGGGHHH!

I DECIDED TO START BY UNDERMINING JABOR'S MORALE. IF THAT DIDN'T WORK, I'D DO SOMETHING SNEAKY.

HOW DOES IT FEEL TO BE INFERIOR TO FAQUARL? I DON'T SEE YOUR MASTER RISKING HIS LIFE IN HERE.

IF I CAN'T TRUST YOU TO LIE DOWN AND DIE WITH THE REST OF THOSE FOOLS AND COWARDS, PERHAPS I SHOULD DISPOSE OF YOU NOW.

RAMUTHRA— THIS BOY MUST DIE FIRST! TAKE HIM!

COWARD! ALWAYS YOU SNEAK AND CRAWL AND RUN!

IT'S CALLED INTELLIGENCE.

KA-ZZZZZT

I feel an alien gaze upon me. My bowels turn to water.

THE SITUATION WAS DETERIORATING RAPIDLY.

AN IDEA CAME INTO MY MIND UNBIDDEN. INTERESTING...

FIRST, THOUGH, I NEEDED TO GET RID OF JABOR.

I GOT INTO POSITION AND, WITH A CHEEKY SMILE, INVITED HIM TO CHARGE.

MY DEAR MASTER SCHYLER SUGGESTED THIS PLAN, AND AS ALWAYS HE WAS INSPIRED. HE WILL BE WATCHING US AT THIS VERY MOMENT.

I DOUBT IT. HE'S LYING DEAD UPSTAIRS.

HE FLEW AT ME IN RAGE.

I SIDESTEPPED HIM AND PUSHED HIM ON TOWARD THE RIFT.

DEAD?

HE WASN'T HAPPY.

HE'D GOTTEN TOO CLOSE AND THE RIFT HAD CAUGHT HIM. LIQUID STREAMS OF GREASY GRAY-BLACK STUFF SPIRALED FROM HIS BODY. THAT WAS HIS ESSENCE GOING.

THAT'S RIGHT, I DIDN'T JUST ESCAPE. I KILLED HIM.

IF HE'D HAD HALF A BRAIN, HE COULD HAVE CHANGED INTO A GNAT OR SOMETHING WITH LESS BULK... BUT HE DIDN'T.

I HAD NO TIME FOR LONG GOOD-BYES. I HAD OTHER MATTERS TO ATTEND TO.

DON'T LIE TO ME, CHILD--

SIMON!

A GREAT HAND REACHED DOWN AND SPED HIM TOWARD SOMETHING THAT MIGHT HAVE BEEN A MOUTH.

AN INSTANT LATER, SIMON LOVELACE WAS GONE.

WELL, THAT WASN'T PRETTY.

NOW ALL WE HAVE TO DO IS GET RID OF BIG BOY OVER THERE. TROUBLE IS, EVEN THE MAGICIANS THAT HAVEN'T BEEN RIPPED IN HALF DON'T LOOK IN A FIT STATE TO RECITE A COMPLEX DISMISSAL SPELL.

I SAW A BRIGHT FIRE OF DETERMINATION IN THE BOY'S EYES.

THE POSSIBILITY THAT IN FACT *I* KNOW THE INCANTATION HADN'T EVEN OCCURRED TO YOU, HAD IT?

ARE YOU SURE? IT'S HIGH LEVEL. AND COMPLEX.

PLUS YOU'LL NEED TO BREAK THE HORN AT EXACTLY THE RIGHT MOMENT.

I'M READY.

I STOOD BACK HELPLESSLY. MY MASTER HELD THE SUMMONING HORN AND CLOSED HIS EYES.

I close my eyes to the chaos in the hall.

That much is easy.

What's hard is shutting out the host of inner voices.

I am always underestimated.

Underwood thought me an imbecile.

Lovelace thought me weak.

Even my own servant, Bartimaeus, doubts I am capable.

Everything is in my hands now.

If I can't bring the spell to mind, more people will die.

They'll die, just as Mrs. Underwood has died.

I feel tears on my cheeks.

I breathe in slowly, and remember...

I remember the garden. I remember the bushes, the leaves, the blossom, the statue...

I remember the spell.

OᒷᒣⅤᒷᒷ!

I speak the words loud and clear and strong.

CRRRRACKKKKK!

With astonishing suddenness, the outline of the demon crumples and shrinks back into the rift.

The tear closes.

Outside, the late afternoon sky is darkening.

And I can hear the wind rushing through the woods.

CHAPTER 42

BARTIMAEUS

TYPICAL OF THE KID, THAT WAS.

CHAPTER 43

SUNSET. THE DAY AFTER THE GREAT SUMMONING.

I PREFERRED YOUR OLD PLACE. THIS ONE SMELLS AND YOU HAVEN'T EVEN MOVED IN YET.

IT DOESN'T SMELL.

THE BOY HAD SPENT ALL DAY WITH MINISTERS AND POLICE, SPINNING AN OUTRAGEOUS YARN ABOUT HOW HE AND HIS POOR DEAD MASTER HAD FOUGHT AGAINST LOVELACE'S EVIL SCHEME.

IT DOES SMELL... OF FRESH PAINT AND PLASTIC AND ALL THINGS NEW. QUITE APPROPRIATE FOR YOU... MR. MANDRAKE.

HE DIDN'T ANSWER. HE WAS BOUNDING OUT TO LOOK AT THE VIEW.

THEY'RE A LOT NEARER FROM HERE.

YES. YOUR MRS. UNDERWOOD WOULD BE PLEASED.

WE FINALLY HAD AN HOUR TO OURSELVES. I INTENDED TO MAKE IT COUNT.

MY NEW MASTER SAYS I HAVE A GREAT CAREER AHEAD OF ME.

AH YES, JESSICA WHITWELL, THE RAKE-THIN MINISTER FOR SECURITY.

I WANT TO WORK AT THE MINISTRY HUNTING THE RESISTANCE. FIRST I'LL CATCH FRED AND STANLEY...AND THAT GIRL. THEN I'LL MAKE THEM TALK...

THE PRIME MINISTER HIMSELF SAID I WAS A HERO.

YEAH? LISTEN. THAT'S THE SOUND OF PEOPLE NOT CHEERING.

THEY HAD TO KEEP IT QUIET FOR SECURITY REASONS.

THEY HAD TO KEEP IT QUIET OR THEY'D LOOK INCREDIBLY STUPID. "TWELVE-YEAR-OLD SAVES GOVERNMENT!" THEY'D HAVE BEEN LAUGHED OFF THE STREETS.

"It's not the commoners that we have to fear. It's the conspirators who got away. Lovelace and Schyler are dead, but we know Lime, the fish-faced one, escaped. And there was at least one more..."

LISTEN, YOU'VE HAD YOUR REVENGE ON LOVELACE. PERHAPS THAT TAKES AWAY A LITTLE OF YOUR PAIN— I HOPE SO.

BUT WE HAD A DEAL. I HELPED YOU, AND I SAVED YOUR LIFE SEVERAL TIMES OVER. NOW IT'S TIME TO HONOR YOUR PROMISE TO LET ME GO...

YES, YOU *DID* HELP ME. YOU *DID* SAVE ME. AND I'M...

EMBARRASSED? DELIGHTED? JUST A TEENSY BIT GRATEFUL?

YES, I'M GRATEFUL, BUT THAT DOESN'T ALTER THE FACT THAT YOU KNOW MY BIRTH NAME.

IF WE'RE BOTH LUCKY, I WON'T BE SUMMONED AGAIN DURING YOUR LIFETIME.

BUT IF I AM— AND IT HURTS ME TO SAY THIS—I PROMISE I WON'T REVEAL YOUR NAME.

I DON'T KNOW. YOU'RE A DEM... A DJINNI. VOWS MEAN NOTHING TO YOU.

DISMISS ME, JOHN. I'VE DONE ENOUGH. I'M TIRED. AND SO ARE YOU.

I'M NOT TIRED. THERE'S A LOT I WANT TO DO.

EXACTLY. YOU'LL WANT A FREE HAND. THINK OF ALL THE OTHER DJINN YOU COULD SUMMON.

THEY WON'T HAVE MY CLASS, BUT THEY'LL GIVE YOU LESS LIP.

ALL RIGHT, BARTIMAEUS. I AGREE.

NATHANIEL— ONE LAST THING. LISTEN, FOR A MAGICIAN, YOU'VE GOT POTENTIAL. YOU HAVE INITIATIVE AND A CONSCIENCE. THEY'RE BOTH RARE AND BOTH EASILY LOST. BE CAREFUL. GUARD THEM... THAT'S ALL.

I'LL BE ALL RIGHT. YOU NEEDN'T BOTHER ABOUT ME.

THE BOY SPOKE THE COUNTER-SUMMONS SWIFTLY AND WITHOUT FAULT.

I FELT THE WEIGHT OF WORDS BINDING ME TO THE EARTH LESSEN WITH EVERY SYLLABLE.

MY FORM EXTENDED AND BLOSSOMED FROM THE CONFINES OF THE CIRCLE.

I ROARED UP AND OUTWARD. THE FINAL BOND BROKE LIKE A SEVERED CHAIN.

SO I DEPARTED, LEAVING BEHIND A PUNGENT SMELL OF BRIMSTONE.

JUST SOMETHING TO REMEMBER ME BY.